The Rainbow Planet

Sister Mary Gundulf

ATHENA PRESS
LONDON

KV-192-761

The Rainbow Planet
Copyright © Sister Mary Gundulf 2005

All Rights Reserved

No part of this book may be reproduced in any form
by photocopying or by any electronic or mechanical means,
including information storage or retrieval systems,
without permission in writing from both the copyright
owner and the publisher of this book.

ISBN 1 84401 422 3

First Published 2005 by
ATHENA PRESS
Queen's House, 2 Holly Road
Twickenham, TW1 4EG
United Kingdom

Printed for Athena Press

ACKNOWLEDGEMENT

— ✦ —

T he author wishes to thank living authors and copyright holders of the books and articles she has quoted or referred to in this book.

ABOUT THE AUTHOR
— ✆ —

S ister Mary Gundulf is a member of the
Anglican Benedictine Community of
nuns at St Mary's Abbey, West Malling,
Kent, England.

INTRODUCTION
— ❦ —

This book about journeys of discovery has been such a journey for the writer. I began with a contemporary version of Bellinda and the Monster. Out of this creative process sprang the first chapter of Part Two, which traces the ancestry of this and similar tales to the myth of the soul's search for the god of love. Then the same father and three daughters took part in the second story of the three tasks in which the sea and the island appear, though they are not in the original myth. The same inspiration led to the second chapter of Part Two, about the sea as it appears in the works of various twentieth-century writers.

From the myth of Eros and Psyche comes the emotive symbol of the water of life, which features in a well-known German tale in the Grimm's collection. In Italo Calvino's Italian collection there is a tale which associates the water of life theme with that of the Sleeping Beauty. I realised that the long, unnatural sleep of that princess derives from the sleep which is the symbol of death in the myth. Psyche is awoken by the prick of Eros's arrow, and I saw in this the origin of the old woman's spindle which sends the sleeping beauty into unconsciousness.

I had expected to go on with another contemporary tale based on a folktale, but found that the third story had to abandon such models, though the same father and daughters appear in this one which connects ancient terrestrial tales with the theme of the exploration of space. Chapter Three of Part Two and four more chapters grew alongside 'The Rainbow Planet'.

Contemporary society is evincing a great need for stories, new and old, in films and books. The same symbols and motifs which helped our primitive ancestors to face initiation ordeals and the surprises of a mysterious and dangerous world can still resonate with us at a very deep level as we encounter the weakening of traditional cultures and institutions and the problems of global pollution and climatic change. Our common enjoyment of such narratives transcends great differences in belief and outlook.

I hope this book will be an enjoyable voyage of discovery for the reader, as it was for the writer, and give some idea of how our reading and viewing can show us meaningful connections, even in the face of increasing chaos. Our compulsion to keep up with the pace of change and the demands of society tends to weaken our conviction of the importance of the inner world which needs stillness and concentration. In this state we resemble Psyche or the Sleeping Beauty in unconsciousness. By heeding myths and tales and the sacred scriptures treasured by our forebears, we can be pricked, so to speak, with love for divine and spiritual things, and the dormant powers of our soul and spirit be awakened and go from strength to strength.

Contents

— ✥ —

Part One

— ❧ —

THE INVISIBLE PALACE

— ❧ —

I t was a wet afternoon and three sisters had somehow to amuse themselves indoors in the sitting room. As the two elder, Mavis and Myrtle, were relatively quiet, the youngest, Rhoda, was able to curl up in an armchair, shut her eyes and enter her palace. It was like the empty palace in fairy tales which conveniently presents itself to the youngest son or daughter, out on their travels, and provides everything they could need.

She, however, thought that such stories were always very short on detail, and was in the habit of exploring and fully visualising her inner palace, whenever a feasible opportunity arose.

To begin with, having left her home and origins far behind, she would be walking through a tremendous forest as dusk was falling, increasingly weary and wondering where to spend the night. Then there would be a great clearing among the trees which was full of mist, forming mysterious shapes. As she stood still and watched, it would take one great form and become solid while she examined it in the dim light.

Being very young, she did not think in terms of architectural styles. Somehow, her palace would combine the best of all kinds of design, without being a graceless hotchpotch. It would not, by the mightiness of its ostentation, make the poor feel out of place. Though of almost unlimited size, it was also cosy and welcoming.

It made use of the stone and wood of the locality, blending harmoniously into its surroundings. While the darkness increased, it became clear that the building had many windows of different shapes and sizes, looking in all directions, as lights appeared inside them, shining out into the night.

The largest light came from the great open door, illuminating the pathway which approached it. She walked up this, with great awe and expectancy, and yet with a sense of ease and familiarity, as she often visited and already belonged here. In the wood owls hooted and foxes barked hoarsely, but there was stillness round the house. Going over the threshold of the great main door was always a risk and a promise, and demanded quiet, relaxed concentration. The door was of wood and stood open for her. Around and above it was grey, ancient stone, and the lintel was carved with illegible letters on scrolls in a dead language, but she knew that their message was welcoming.

The entrance hall was large and stately with a high, vaulted ceiling and a floor covered with black and white marble squares. The walls were panelled with wood and sconces at intervals gave light. At the opposite side to the way she had entered, an inner door stood ajar. Soft light shone through the opening and Rhoda could hear wonderful music floating gently towards her. The palace was empty. There was no one to be seen, but the music was like a welcoming voice. She crossed the hall and went through the door. Here was a warm room with a carpet, curtains at the windows, and an open fire of logs which flamed and glowed.

The music, played on an invisible flute by invisible hands, became quieter and ceased, leaving a soothing silence behind it. All round the room, a series of paintings hung on the walls, apparently depicting different episodes in the same story. There were three girls in them, rather like herself and her two sisters. Rhoda did not take in much at first glance. She was tired and hungry, and a table stood before the fire with an attractive supper laid out on it. She sat down and ate and drank. Dishes were removed and replaced by invisible hands and drinks poured out, but she saw no one. As she ate, she sat opposite a painting of a wild mountain at dusk with a moon rising and a maiden on top of it, looking lonely and afraid, but she paid it little attention.

When she had finished supper, the table was cleared and various games and puzzles were placed on it. Rhoda played several kinds of Patience which she knew, using a pack of beautiful cards, and then began a jigsaw puzzle of St George and the Dragon, with the maiden standing by. By the time she had completed the more interesting parts of this, with the brightest colours, she was very sleepy and it felt late. She picked up a candle which had been left on the table for her and found a different door from the one she had entered by. It led into a passage at the end of which she found a stone staircase spiralling upwards. This ended at a door which opened straight into a turret chamber, round and rather small, with tapestries on the walls and a curtained bed. Rhoda made pretty short work of her ablutions at a washstand with a flower-patterned basin and ewer upon it and soon climbed into bed.

She slept soundly and long and woke much refreshed to hear birds singing in chorus outside the window. She got up and drew back the curtain from the lattice and looked at the palace grounds. The clearing in the great forest was extensive and the palace stood in formal gardens, beautifully kept. The one thing Rhoda now wanted was to be in those gardens, so she dressed and went down and found an outside door from the passage at the bottom of the stairs.

First there was a paved patio with seats looking out. A low stone balustrade edged it, with statues at intervals. These were mostly of animals such as hares and squirrels, and large birds with their wings partly unfurled. Beyond the pavement, a path led under an arbour with scented trailing plants growing over it. On either side were beds of herbs and aromatic plants, with smaller paths among them. Rhoda crossed the patio and walked down the long path slowly, taking deep breaths of wonderfully scented air. The mysterious essence of the deserted yet friendly garden seemed to enter her and pervade her being with the vital air. She came to a place where the path opened out to a circular paved area. Opposite it continued and another path very like it crossed at this point, making left and right turnings.

In the middle of the circle was a magnificent rose tree, covered with silky, pale yellow blossoms. Rhoda knew that her name meant rose in Greek, and she felt that the flowers were mainly there for her benefit. As she had taken food and sleep indoors with impunity, there seemed no reason why she should not pick one perfect rose, just opening from a bud. She stood still and carefully selected one. As she broke its stem from the tree, there was a startling hiss and a ferocious Dragon head reared up among the blooms on a long, sinuous neck, covered with shining green scales. It flapped huge, webbed wings, brandished claws and breathed out fire and smoke with a foul smell of sulphur which poisoned the atmosphere, drowning all scents.

'How dare you steal my roses, little girl?' it hissed menacingly.

'I beg your pardon, sir. I didn't know they were yours. My name is Rhoda, which means rose.'

'You are my prisoner now, little rose. You must live in my palace forever,' said the monster, eyeing her hungrily.

Rhoda was nearly overpowered by the sulphurous fumes by this time. 'Yes, sir, certainly sir,' she gasped, curtseying as steadily as she could with faintness upon her. The monster closed its wings, coiled up its neck and lowered itself out of sight among the roses. Fragrant breezes soon dispersed the sulphurous stink and made Rhoda feel better. She pinned the rose to her dress in front and walked on. She continued along the path opposite the one she had come down until stone steps led her to a sunken pool. A fountain played gently in the centre of it, making a soothing sound. The day was hot now, and the cool look of the water most appealing. Rhoda sat down on a seat from which one could see into the pool and began to relax after her fright.

Now that the Dragon had disappeared and did not seem to be following her, she was inclined to think her adventure only made the palace garden a more interesting and varied place. She grew still, and various birds took courage to perch on the brink of the water and take sips. A song thrush was performing cheerfully on a willow tree nearby, which added to her reassurance. Her heart stopped thumping, her breathing deepened and a wonderful peace stole gradually into her. Her eyes were closed when she seemed to hear, mingled with the plash of the fountain, a hint of music. At first it was a single, rich, bell-like note, reverberating from the depths of the pool. Presently a higher note answered it, with a flute-like quality. After a while, as many as five higher notes were sounded, in permutations and combinations rather than melodies, with the faint deep note continuing as a drone below them.

At first Rhoda was content just to enjoy this, concentrating on each sound and forgetting past and future. In the end she became curious to know how such strangely disembodied music could proceed out of water when no performer or instrument was visible.

She got up and walked gently to the brink. Coloured fishes darted among flowing weeds. No bottom could be seen. The water might be very deep. She looked up at the fountain and was amazed to notice that the rising and falling water drops were assuming a shape, graceful and mobile, which seemed increasingly human in appearance. She looked as steadily as she could at so much twinkling and shimmering. As she watched, the whiteness of water became pale skin and the changing outlines settled into one beautiful, slender form which detached itself from the fountain and moved slowly towards Rhoda. By now the music had ceased and there was only the sound of falling water.

'Do you like my pool, little girl?' the water-lady asked her.

'I love it,' she answered, smiling.

'Are you happy in your palace?'

'Is it *my* palace?' asked Rhoda doubtfully.

'Whose else could it be?'

'I met a Dragon as I came through the garden who said it was his palace and that I was his prisoner.'

'A place this size must have many inhabitants besides yourself,' said the lady.

Rhoda thought about this. 'I'm glad I've found you here, anyway,' she said. 'You make me feel better, and I love your water music.'

The white lady laughed. 'If ever you're lonely and afraid, princess, come down to my pool and wait for me,' she said. Rhoda looked into her kindly face, but while she gazed, mist and water drops began to obscure its features and the whole white form became nebulous. After a while it was assimilated into the waters of the fountain, but Rhoda felt that a friendly presence remained all round her and was not distressed. Presently she rose and began walking back through the garden. She did not wish to pass the fateful rose tree in the centre of the four main walks, so skirted the garden by smaller paths, among a great variety of plants and flowers.

— ✖ —

'What are you thinking about, Ro?' Mavis had brought the problems of her maths homework to a satisfactory conclusion and now sought a diversion.

'Who wants to hear that again?' asked Myrtle scornfully, intent on fine embroidery. 'It's bound to be her creepy old palace with no one in it and some sort of devil at the bottom of the garden.'

'You needn't listen, Myr,' said Mavis with authority. 'I want to know, Ro. Really I do,' she went on. 'Tell me what happened this time.'

Rhoda had jumped at this sudden interruption, not recognising at first where it could have come from. Mavis, when in the mood, was not a bad listener, however, so she began from when she had approached the palace through the forest at evening and told of her experiences in the garden next day.

Now Rhoda had brought Mavis abreast with events up till she began wandering in the outskirts of the garden after leaving the pool. Though inclined to be sceptical as a rule, Mavis had to admit on this occasion that the garden was of an overwhelming loveliness and full of a most intriguing atmosphere of enchantment. As a result, the two sisters were able to go on together, following winding paths between glorious, scented blossoms of all colours. By the time they approached the palace again the sun was westering and it was becoming cooler. Rhoda had almost forgotten her anxiety to avoid the area of the rose tree and its alarming guardian. They found themselves approaching the paved terrace by another route and Mavis admired the lifelike statues of animals and birds which seemed about to transcend the immobility of stone and begin frisking or flying around.

They re-entered the building by the small door Rhoda had used to come out in the morning. She began showing her sister some of the beauties of the rooms, but both were hungry and rather tired by this time, and when they entered the room where

Rhoda had eaten the evening before, they were delighted to find a wonderful supper spread out on the table. Rhoda invited Mavis to join her and they sat down while the invisible flute began to play in a festive manner and unseen hands ministered to their needs as they ate and drank.

They had not long finished their supper and sat relaxed holding glasses in which a little wine remained, chatting to one another, when suddenly the flute music broke off and was succeeded by a roll of drums suggesting thunder which made them sit up in surprise. The door from the hall opened and the fearful Dragon of the rose tree burst in.

'Had a good supper, little rose?' he inquired in the manner of a good host.

'Yes, sir, thank you, sir. It was excellent,' said Rhoda nervously.

'And who are you?' he roared, glaring at Mavis. 'Did I invite you to my palace?' The older sister was usually self-possessed in any situation, but now she merely gaped at the Dragon in open horror which was not calculated to appease him. So Rhoda answered:

'This is Mavis, my oldest sister. She's not good at enchantments like this, but she's good at maths and things like that. She finished her homework and interrupted me, so I had to bring her back with me.'

Myrtle got up and shook Mavis by the shoulders. 'Mavis, you idiot, I told you not to listen to Ro's daft stories. Look at the fright you're in! It's worse than a nightmare.' Mavis uncharacteristically shuddered and said nothing. Rhoda, looking round, found that Mavis was no longer at the table with her, but had left her alone with the monster.

'Your sister didn't like the look of me,' he said, aggrieved. 'Am I so ghastly to look at? Do you want to run home?'

'You're first rate as Dragons go,' said Rhoda carefully.

'Will you marry me then, dear little rose?' he asked wistfully, restraining the fire of his breath and trying not to poison the air with sulphur.

'I'm afraid I couldn't do that, sir,' she answered, trying to sound reasonably courteous.

'All the same, stay in my palace and you shall have all you

desire,' he said and went out by the way he came in. Rhoda stayed in the palace and gardens for many days, finding much to interest and divert her. In the evening she always found her supper laid out on the table, and when she had finished the Dragon never failed to appear. He asked kindly after her welfare and she became used to his alarming appearance. He always asked for her hand in marriage, but she put him off discreetly without giving offence.

As the monster only seemed able to appear and talk to her in the evenings, Rhoda began to be rather lonely in the long days and to wish she had someone to share her interests and exciting discoveries. One day she found a pavement in a distant part of the grounds which was covered with obscure mathematical diagrams, with words in a language she could not understand. As she gazed at it in puzzled frustration, she wished Mavis could be there with her, as it was the sort of thing she might be able to explain. That night, when the Dragon had entered the supper room, Rhoda asked whether she could visit her home for a while and then return. He appeared hurt and said, 'Aren't you happy in my palace any longer?'

'I'm very happy,' she tried to explain. 'And I want to tell Mavis about it. I feel lonely sometimes,' she added, 'and I miss my sisters.'

The Dragon nodded sadly. 'You will have to go to your old home, little rose, but it is dangerous. If you forget me, I shall become ill. You must take something with you to remind you that you belong here.'

'I won't forget you, sir,' she answered, 'but I'd like something to remember you by.'

The Dragon produced a gold ring with a clear crystal set on it.

'Take this,' he said. 'As long as the crystal is clear I am well, but if you see it cloud over I shall be pining for you. Hurry back, or I cannot recover.'

— ❧ —

Rhoda went to bed in her turret chamber with the ring on the third finger of her right hand. Next day she awoke in her ordinary bedroom at home. Rain was pouring outside the window and thick clouds made the light dim and dreary. She was engulfed by dreadful gloom, such as one feels after coming back from a gorgeous holiday which has gone too fast. She put her head back under the bedclothes and felt anxiously for the ring on her right hand, to make sure her monster was not only a dream. There it was, smooth, solid and cold to the touch. She pulled back the bedclothes to make sure the crystal looked clear, hoping the monster did not already feel as desperate as she did. It was brighter than anything in her dull, ordinary bedroom. The contrast was too much, and I am sorry to say that, being only very young, she burst into tears of hearty self-pity. After a while the door opened and in came Mavis, in her red dressing gown.

'Look who's here!' she said. 'You don't seem very pleased to be back with us.' Then her eye travelled from Rhoda to the table by the bed. 'Whatever have you got there?'

Rhoda looked at the table and noticed for the first time that there were three mysterious parcels of funny shapes there.

Mavis reached the table with alacrity and found that one parcel had a label attached saying 'Mavis'. She sat down on the bed and took Rhoda in her arms. Since their mother's death in Rhoda's babyhood, Mavis, who was a good deal older, had been something of a substitute.

'Do open your parcel, Mavis,' Rhoda said.

'I can't do it if you're howling your head off. It spoils the atmosphere.'

'I'm all right now,' Rhoda replied. She still felt shattered but curiosity was stronger and the parcels came from her palace. Mavis turned to the table again, but at that moment the door burst open and in rushed Myrtle.

'Here's a present for you, Myr,' said Mavis, noticing that a second parcel had a label saying 'Myrtle'.

'Oh, I say,' said Myrtle sarcastically. 'Aren't we the posh little lady, whisked back by magic at the dead of night and comes with pretty parcels to make us sweet!' All the same, she came up to the table and gazed at it with interest.

'There's one for Dad too. Shall I get him before we open them?' she asked. She turned to the door, but it opened at once and their father appeared, having heard the commotion in the house.

'Isn't it touching, Dad? Our dear little sister has flitted back to us with presents from the fairy palace. Who's going to open one first?' Myrtle said, failing to conceal a certain excitement.

Their father's thin face was lined with worry and his sparse hair was greying. With no wife to help him, three young daughters were a heavy demand and his financial affairs had sadly declined since he had started out as a promising young businessman.

'Everybody get dressed, quick, and we'll have the presents at the breakfast table,' he announced firmly. There was a general howl from all the sisters, but he ignored it. 'I'll never get to the office if we stand here talking. Everybody downstairs in five minutes,' he said and left the room, carrying the three mysterious packages with him. Galvanised by curiosity, they all tumbled into their clothes and raced down to the dining room.

It was agreed that Mavis should open her parcel first. When the dull-coloured wrappings fell aside, an object of amazing brilliance was revealed. It was obviously mathematical in some way, as circles and triangles and other shapes could be glimpsed within it, in complicated interaction. Though golden it was transparent, and seemed to glow with a light from its own centre. It made Mavis feel distinctly uncomfortable.

'What's this, Rho?' she asked sharply. 'What am I supposed to do with it?'

'I've never seen it before,' Rhoda said, 'but I don't think you use it exactly. If you just look at it, it might show you things about maths and all that. Your sort of things.'

It was not necessary to tell Mavis to look at her gift, since she held it as though it stuck to her. Her gaze was riveted upon it, but she appeared more alarmed than pleased. She was unusually silent. Now it was Myrtle's turn. Her parcel was bright red and when opened revealed a golden coloured box. She lifted the lid, expecting gorgeous jewellery to be within, but there was another box exactly fitting inside, which was silver in colour. Looking slightly disappointed, she lifted its lid, only to see a third box, of a dull grey. Her expression was becoming indignant, but curiosity held her. She opened the third box and saw nothing but folds of white material. Searching among them, she found a single, wizened walnut shell.

'Is this a joke?' she exploded at last.

'Crack the nut,' suggested Rhoda. Their father, with an eye on the time, produced a pair of nutcrackers with alacrity and Myrtle carefully cracked the nut without splintering the shell. She took the top half off and there, cradled in the other, was something made of incredibly fine silk. Roused to interest, she removed it gently and unfolded a gown of breathtaking beauty, shimmering with a multitude of subtle shades of colour which appeared and re-formed as the material was moved. Myrtle stared, dumbfounded.

'Aren't you going to wear it?' asked Rhoda.

'Yes, let's see you in it, dear,' said Father, trying to hide a certain impatience.

Like a sleepwalker, Myrtle put the dress over her head and groped for the armholes, but the gown which had fitted into the tiny shell was many sizes too big and enveloped her completely.

'You'll have to grow into a woman before you can wear that, dear,' Father said. 'Put it away again in its shell and all the boxes.' Myrtle looked like crying at this, so Rhoda helped take it off gently and the capacious gown went easily back into its small compass again.

'Now it's my turn,' their father said. His parcel was green and when unwrapped, revealed a large, ancient, leather-bound book. 'What time does your friend think I've got for reading?' he muttered, but he was intrigued. He opened the book, but the writing was in a language he could not recognise and even the alphabet was strange to him. There were many beautiful hand-painted illustrations in amazing colours, showing beasts and plants, but these were all unrecognisable. 'It's a rare book. I must get an expert to value it,' he said, rising quickly from the table. 'I must go now,' he added, and went off in his usual weekday whirl, but it was clear that he felt somehow disconcerted.

— ✑ —

It was school holidays so the girls had all day before them. Mavis and Myrtle had a project in the small back garden for making a fish pond. They asked Rhoda to help. It was messy work involving digging and removing soil. Mavis saw the gold and crystal ring on Rhoda's hand and offered to keep it safe and clean for her. Rhoda disliked being parted from it, but Mavis was firm that such a treasure must not be dirtied. Later, when they came in for lunch, Rhoda asked for the ring back, but Mavis pleaded for a chance to wear it on her hand. Rhoda could not refuse, though she thought Mavis might have been content with her own present from the Dragon. This, however, with the other presents, was shut away in a cupboard.

Days passed and Mavis gave the ring to Myrtle for a turn at wearing it. Later, Rhoda noticed that neither of them wore it and was worried but they complained of her meanness if she clamoured for its return. Meanwhile, they examined it in secret and were surprised that the crystal began losing its clarity and became dark and cloudy. Each thought privately that this might be a reflection on her own moral character. Perhaps it was a magic ring which darkened with the sins of a wearer? They hid it away and parried Rhoda's questions, but eventually her concern for the Dragon and his welfare overcame all the inferiority she felt towards her two forceful sisters and she insisted on hunting for the ring in their rooms. When she discovered it at last and saw how it was changed, she was distraught and announced that she must return to the Dragon at once.

She had never found the journey long or difficult before, but now everything contributed to discourage and weary her. Rain fell in sheets so that she could hardly see the signposts. When she reached the forest, she followed endless paths which were almost overgrown with nettles and brambles. It grew darker and darker, wolves howled in the distance and the wind roared and moaned alternately. When she at last reached the clearing where the palace stood, clouds scudded in front of a sickle moon, hiding most of its feeble light. The palace was dark. Not a light shone anywhere and the outline of the roofs against the moonlit sky was more like that of a long-abandoned ruin than an inhabited dwelling place. She went up to the main door, which swung on its hinges in the wind. As she entered, there was no welcoming music, but the high, thin wailing of the gale. She went to the room where she had eaten, but there was no fire in the grate or meal on the table. She wandered from room to room in search of her former host, to see if he lay sick anywhere, but most rooms upstairs were empty or locked, and dust lay everywhere.

In the end, almost too weary to put one foot in front of another, she left the house to search the grounds by the diminishing sunlight. She called and called and no one answered. At last she remembered the kind water-woman who had told her to seek her help if she was in trouble, so she went down to the sunken pool far from the house. The darkness was almost impenetrable here, but she heard the splash of the fountain. She approached the edge and leant over, stretching out her hands to feel the falling drops, though she was soaked through already and the water felt freezing cold. Suddenly she started back, as a huge shape loomed up, a long sinuous body swimming fast, with a fierce head reared up on the end, opening huge jaws full of teeth, as though it would devour her. She staggered back, as it leant out after her, but regained her balance. The serpent withdrew its head, being apparently confined to the watery element, hissing disgustedly.

Rhoda was so terrified at this, that she forgot about avoiding the fateful rosebush at the centre of two broad walks.

She approached it slowly, as she returned from the pond, faint with hunger and exhaustion. Rain still fell and wind beat against her, but as she was passing the big bush, the moon shone out among the black clouds and showed her a huge shape lying under it. She went up to it in terror, wondering if it was another serpent, but the form never stirred. At last she plucked up courage to lean right over its head, and heard faint, rasping breaths and caught a whiff of sulphur. She felt rather sick, but whispered, 'Is it you, sir? What can I do to save you?'

So faint that she could hardly hear came the answer, 'I need a rose.' Rhoda looked up at the bush above them, but all the roses were dead and there were nothing but thorns. Then she remembered the significance of her name.

'The only rose here is me, sir,' she said sadly. The Dragon made no reply but lay inert. The wind howled wretchedly and Rhoda shivered in her wet clothes.

'Dear Dragon,' she said slowly and clearly, as he already seemed far away from her. 'If only you will get better and stand up I will marry you at once and love you for ever.' At this she heard noises from behind. When she turned she saw animals running towards her and birds flying. She recognised them as the ones she had seen in stone on pedestals on the patio. She gasped in amazement but looked back hurriedly towards the rosebush. The Dragon's vast form had completely disappeared. Where it had lain stood a boy about her own age.

'Where is the Dragon?' she asked him with some indignation.

'Here,' said the boy, smiling cheerfully. 'I was under enchantment and had to look like that till a girl said she would marry me as I was.' Then Rhoda realised that she was enriched and not deprived by the boy's appearance.

'Oh, look at the palace!' she exclaimed. It had regained its inhabited, welcoming look, with lights at the windows, and as many different festal tunes floating out as if it had been a college of music.

'Race you there!' shouted the jubilant boy, and they dashed towards it neck and neck, with a crowd of animals and birds keeping pace, squeaking and roaring in chorus. When they arrived, Rhoda was amazed and delighted to see her father at the great door, looking completely relaxed and leisured. He opened his arms wide to receive her and showed equal delight at meeting the boy whom he at once addressed as his son.

THE UNKNOWN ISLAND
— ❦ —

Rhoda, Myrtle and Mavis were sitting with their father in the dining room of the Sea-View Hotel at a most ordinary resort. The white tablecloths were ordinary and so were the knives and forks and the bottles of sauce and ketchup. The evening meal, which was larger and greasier than meals at home, and rather heavy weather for the stomach, seemed to consist mostly of chipped potatoes, drowned in profundities of deep fat. It was wonderful of Dad to afford the money or the time to bring his daughters to the seaside for a week's holiday. The girls knew it was their duty to enjoy themselves and be agreeable when he was around, but it was all rather heavy going. Like the chips.

There were a number of other tables with families like themselves in the dining room and a subdued and civilised murmur of conversation. By now they more or less knew all the other guests by sight and there was nothing very remarkable about any of them. Suddenly the door to the dining room from the hotel hall opened with more than its usual energy and a woman stepped in who, for some reason they could not quite have explained, at once riveted the three girls' attention. Their father was sitting with his back to the new arrival, manfully plodding through a large dish of greasy eggs and chips, liberally bespattered with Worcester sauce, so did not see her, but he became aware of a certain alertness round the table.

A waiter stepped up to the woman and appeared to suggest a table, but after a brief exchange, he indicated theirs and, to their immense surprise, she then bore down upon them. There happened to be two superfluous chairs there, as it was really a table for six, so the family could not deny that there was room for this intruder. She smiled sweetly at them all and said, 'Do you mind if I join you?' in such a beguiling manner that they suddenly felt it would be boorish to refuse.

'I've often seen you three lovely girls on the beach,' she went on, as she seated herself. The waiter bustled up and laid a place for her. 'I've got a little boat I go out in. You might like to join me some time.'

As her gaze flashed upon them in turn, they were aware of sparkling bright green eyes and shimmering, silky attire in which various shades of blue, green and turquoise came and went with her graceful movements and the play of light, which seemed to have a greater intensity around her than anywhere else in the room. When her dinner arrived they saw an amazing collection of outlandish seafood set upon a bed of fresh seaweed. To gaze at it was to imagine oneself fathoms down in an ocean full of forms and colours foreign to Earth and land. How such a plateful could possibly be cajoled out of the management of this most plebeian hotel they could not imagine.

The lady tackled this collection with a most elegant enthusiasm while showing great conversational skill. She talked to Dad about business in such a way that new and adventurous ideas arose which seemed to him to be his own invention, yet he certainly had had no such inspiration before she began drawing him out.

She spoke to the girls about their holiday and their interests in such a way that it suddenly seemed like the most promising and thrilling opportunity of their whole lives. The sea ceased to be a bit of wet stuff on the edge of the beach and seemed instead the enchanted threshold to a whole new world of experience capable of turning them all inside out.

Before they had finished the various shades of ice cream which followed their first course, they were looking forward to meeting the lady on the seashore next day. The thought of actually going out in her small boat on the water made them almost breathless with anticipation and excitement, as though an entry was to be granted them to a new and greatly superior dimension of reality. When supper was over they all went out together on to the beach. The tide was out and the murmur of the waves sounded sleepy and distant. A moon was reflected in the water, catching the foam at the edges of the waves and making it gleam in the dim light. They said goodbye to the lady outside the hotel and she promised to meet them in the morning.

The girls woke painfully early and did not know how to stay in their dull hotel beds till breakfast in the dining room, which seemed to start disgustingly late. Father was incredibly calm, waking late and wasting about an hour, or so it seemed, in getting dressed and shaved.

Unadorned by the fabulous lady, the dining table was a place of incredible monotony. The girls nearly choked on platefuls of porridge and kippers. They were far too excited to be hungry, but Father plodded systematically through the meal and refused to be rushed. The toast, served in triangles, was intolerably dry and made them cough. Only the grapefruit with a cherry in the middle slipped down more easily, and the coffee was stimulating. At long last when the sun was high and the best part of the morning seemed already to be over, Father put on his sunhat and beach shoes and declared himself to be at their disposal. When they reached the beach it was crowded with families in deck chairs and people and dogs in all directions. They could not see the lady or her boat and wandered about, finding life increasingly tedious.

They made their way to the edge of the water, to get a clearer view. The tide was quite high now, covering most of the sand and stirring the seaweed stranded by a previous high tide. A long way off they caught sight of a group of small boats drawn up on the sand, so they began walking towards them, at the edge of the breaking waves. At last they left the crowds behind and arrived at the empty vessels. They were beautiful little crafts, full of gear and tackle and redolent of aquatic adventures, but there was no sign of the lady, or of any other boat owner. The girls were most taken with one called *Ocean Star*, painted white with green and blue furnishings. As they looked at her, something of the stimulus of the green lady's presence at supper last night returned to them and they stood dreaming of bobbing on the waves and leaving a gleaming wake behind them. Eventually, however, they were tired of standing about and began wandering back along the beach, thinking of other diversions the resort town might offer to compensate for their disappointment. There was lunch to think of, for one thing, and the sea air and exercise had made this interesting. Also, there was a large funfair in full swing which they had not yet visited.

By the time they had been on a few roundabouts, Mavis and Myrtle had forgotten about the lady and her boat. The enjoyment of the moment engrossed them. Rhoda, however, found that whizzing round on a wooden horse or motorbike had lost its charm. Images of sand and seashells and waving weed kept floating before her inner eye. Without the sparkling company of the green lady, life seemed aimless and depressing. Wandering away from her sisters, who were consuming great clouds of pink candyfloss on sticks and laughing hysterically as it coated their faces, she went among various tents containing sideshows and amusements. She was standing at some distance from a hoop-la, when she noticed a movement at the side of her vision. Perhaps some animal had gone round the back of the tent. She walked round quietly so as to get a look without alarming whatever it was.

There was nothing close to the tent, but she thought she detected another movement at the edge of the fairground, behind a tree. She crept towards the place very cautiously and was amazed to see a very small man looking round a tree trunk and beckoning vigorously. His face and hands were brown with exposure to air and sun, and deeply wrinkled. He wore dark blue trousers and a sailor's jersey. When he saw that Rhoda was following him without hesitation he came out on a path and went ahead of her. After a while, the way went down steeply, zigzagging across a hill, until it emerged by the sea at a small harbour which Rhoda had never seen, though she thought she had often explored the whole place. A few boats were drawn up by a jetty and among them Rhoda at once recognised the white one she had seen earlier at the other end of the beach. As the sun caught it, it acquired a sheen like mother-of-pearl. There was still no sign of the lady who had come to their hotel last night, but the sight of the boat brought the memory of her powerfully back to Rhoda. As she stood gazing, the small man, hardly taller than she was, stood beside her.

'Do you know the lady we met last night?' she asked him.

He did not seem to understand English. Perhaps he was a foreigner. He only pointed to the boat, then to her, took her hand and indicated by signs that they should go down to it. Rhoda was very willing, so they walked out on the jetty and were soon alongside the enticing vessel, bobbing gently on a slight swell. Apart from themselves, the whole place was oddly deserted and utterly silent. The dwarf looked at her, jumped aboard, and definitely beckoned her to follow. She did not know whether it would be a ride, or just an inspection of the boat at its moorings, but she felt complete confidence in the little man and was sure he must be a servant of her green lady, even if he could not say so in words. As he brought the boat close alongside the jetty, she stepped into it nimbly, then found it was safer to sit down quickly on the nearest seat, as her arrival caused a certain amount of rocking, light as she was.

In a moment, the dwarf had a green sail up which bellied gently in an off-shore breeze. He also started a motor and under the double power, the boat shot out of the harbour in a matter of seconds and was away at a splendid speed across the open sea. Rhoda was surprised, but thrilled. How much better this was than whizzing round on a silly roundabout with her sisters! Of course, she'd like them to come on a ride like this some other time, but at present it was wonderful to have her own adventure. The dwarf had to sit facing the way they were going and steer, so she was opposite him, facing the receding land and admiring the fine, straight wake they made, as the moving water caught the sunlight and sparkled with sudden rainbow colours, like a spray of diamonds.

Their speed remained steady for hours, as the afternoon wore on. Rhoda became aware of a waxing moon rising in the east on her right and gaining in height and brightness. On the opposite side of the sky, the sun was declining behind banks of clouds which changed shape quickly, suggesting all sorts of faces, creatures, towers and palaces. Presently they were lit by sunset colours, which were also reflected in the sea, in a great road towards the west, like a royal progress covered with red carpet. All shades of orange, peach, pink and crimson were there in increasing intensity, like a swelling chorus of colour which was almost audible. When the colour finally drained away, it seemed to leave a peaceful, sleepy hush over the air and water. The west ceased to command attention, and now it was drawn to the other side of the boat where a path of silver led over the gentle swell towards the ascending moon. The moonlight, too, seemed full of silent melody. As Rhoda looked along the sea road, she discerned a gigantic feminine figure, shaped from silver sheen. It approached with effortless, gliding steps till it towered over the boat, which seemed like a tiny toy by contrast.

'So you're coming to my island, Rhoda?' said a grand, congenial voice. 'That is the place for you. You have work there.' Rhoda recognised in these tones the voice of the lady who had met them in the hotel. At the same time, she experienced the sound as if it were within her somewhere. She felt very small beside the huge figure of cosmic proportions, its head in the sky, and yet totally empowered by it, as though capable of heroic feats. The dwarf steered the boat towards the lady, who moved off over the waves before them. Rhoda turned to look the way they were going and saw a dark mass of land looming against the silver light. As the moon declined it disappeared behind a great cliff and the silver road on the water vanished with it. Rhoda no longer saw the colossal figure as the little sailor steered, as it seemed, straight towards solid rock. Sharp, mossy shapes were looming right over them when the boat entered a sea-filled cavern. The sound of the waves against their vessel echoed in the hollow space around them.

Rhoda's state of exaltation diminished considerably as the sides of the cavern drew closer until the boat was negotiating a dark tunnel. The dwarf was no longer using sail or engine, but sculling cautiously along with a single oar, perhaps avoiding dangerous rocks under the surface. As the darkness increased the small boatman produced a large electric torch from a shelf beside him and handed it to Rhoda, indicating that she should shine it the way they were going. Soon a flight of stone steps appeared leading up from the water and near them a large iron ring fastened in the rock. Rhoda kept the light on this and the dwarf brought the boat up and passed the painter through the ring, so as to make it fast. Then he took the torch and got out at the foot of the step, turning to light her landing after him. Then he went up the rough stair cut in rock ahead and motioned for her to follow.

Rhoda found the place somewhat foreboding, but could not stay alone in the dark. The damp, rather slippery steps had a certain fascination, making her wonder where they might lead. They went up and up till she was weary, without coming out of the great cavern. At last the stair ended on a platform outside a large wooden door, studded with nails. This struck her as looking most like the entrance to a dungeon, which was a bit daunting, but the dwarf turned the large iron ring which served for a handle and pushed the door open. He led the way inside a vast chamber, very dim but apparently all of stone, including the ceiling. A little daylight or moonlight fell from a small opening high up somewhere. As Rhoda stepped forward she felt small, hard objects under her feet. She looked down and saw that the torchlight showed various kinds of seeds and grains scattered about on the floor. She began picking up and examining different kinds and found wheat, barley, millet, poppy seeds, peas, beans and lentils. Then she noticed a huge pile of these, all hopelessly mixed up together.

The dwarf had not spoken. He had only stood and shone the torch on the pile, but she knew, as though by a regal command from the tremendous lady who had led them to her island home, that she must impose order on all this chaos, or she would never penetrate the place further or have any peace of mind. At the same time, the complete impossibility of the task was evident, especially as she knew there was a time limit of a few hours. She was not surprised when the dwarf handed the torch to her and went out, locking the great door. As there was nothing to be done about the situation, and she was tired from the journey, she sat down, put the torch out and began daydreaming. She saw, in a series of vivid mental pictures, the immense potential of all that seed. There were golden cornfields in the sun, the grain full of flowers in bloom, poppies, cornflowers, moon daisies, corn cockle, sorrel, vetch and many others. Bees hummed contentedly among them and butterflies fluttered above, alighting here and there. Peas grew high on wooden supports, waving white flowers, and there were acres of vigorous bean plants with different colour blooms.

All this was marvellous to contemplate, but did not advance her immediate task. Sitting in the near darkness, she became aware of movement. She looked about her and the scattered grains and pulses seemed to be moving about in a strange way, not randomly, but as though directed. Peering around, she saw that the big heap had diminished and smaller heaps spaced round the large floor had appeared. She was sure they had not been there at first.

As she looked, the big heap grew smaller and she made out as many as seven other piles; one, presumably, for each of the seven varieties she had identified, but it was too dark to see. She did not like to switch the torch on suddenly, in case it introduced confusion into such a wonderfully orderly process.

At last she managed to see that little black legs protruded under the seeds as they moved on their way. She next made out the heads and bodies of thousands of ants, all working on her behalf, as though directed by a single intelligence.

She sat until the dawn light from the window grew strong enough to see the completed task. No little running legs were visible any more. The scene was one of satisfying orderliness. Rhoda felt as though it was she who had achieved the solution of inner chaos. There was one pile in the centre of dark poppy seed. Around it at regular intervals were the wheat nearest the window, peas next going round clockwise, then barley and beans opposite the wheat. After these were millet and lentils, thus:

wheat

lentils   peas

poppy

millet   barley

beans

An equilateral triangle of grains overlay an identical one of pulses making a star, with flower seeds in the centre of the figure. Looking round, Rhoda saw a mattress in a corner with a bed made up for sleeping. She did not need a poppy seed to induce her to lie down at once, overwhelmed with satisfying fatigue, as though she, not the ants, had laboured creatively all night.

She slept continuously for some hours and awoke full of curiosity to explore her surroundings and find the further task she felt sure would await her in the lady's stronghold.

There was now more light in the place. As well as the window, sunshine came from a door at the top of a flight of steps, opposite where she had entered. This door now stood open. Rhoda did not know whether it had been closed last night, or open but dark beyond. Now she got up and climbed the rough, rock-hewn steps. When she went through the heavy wooden door, she found a pool of clear water in which she bathed and a table with food and drink at which she had breakfast. Feeling restored and respectable, she continued along a sort of gallery until she came to an opening which gave a long view of the country. The sun was high in the sky and there were meadows beside a stream.

The light fell on something golden and she saw large, fierce looking sheep and rams, with fleeces full of dazzling reflected light.

Rhoda knew she must have some of that wool, and that this must be the second task she was appointed to accomplish. As she began the descent from the rocky stronghold down a steep path, she heard crashes and saw that the horned rams were charging each other with great force. When she at last reached the level of the fields where they were grazing, or fighting, some of the animals caught sight of her and looked as though they meant to charge. Rhoda was alarmed and perplexed. She made for the nearest cover, a group of trees and bushes growing beside the stream. The sheep lost interest when she was out of sight. She could see them through the branches and keep an eye on their movements. Even so, she found her heart was thumping and she was shaking all over in a way that made her feel ashamed. A brave adventuress should not react like this, she felt, and tried to relax and take deep breaths while she thought what to do next. Then her ear caught a beautiful sound.

It was the music of a small pipe, simple and repetitious, but she found it profoundly soothing and reassuring. She went toward the sound, keeping carefully among the bushes, and saw a small island in midstream, on which a boy was sitting and playing. She wondered how to reach him, then noticed a row of stepping stones sticking out of the shallow water. The boy stopped playing as she approached him and smiled a welcome.

'What shall I do about the sheep?' Rhoda asked him at once.

It seemed obvious that he would know the answer to anything.

'I must have some of that golden wool, but they are too dangerous.'

'Wait for the siesta,' the boy replied. 'After midday, they all lie down and go to sleep. Nothing wakes them for hours.'

He then resumed playing his reed pipe and Rhoda sat on soft, mossy grass and listened. The sun rose to the zenith as shadows grew minimal. The heat increased and everything was quiet. She no longer heard the bleating and fighting of the sheep. She thanked the boy and crossed on the stones to look through the bushes. Every one of the large animals lay resplendent in the sunshine. The light from their fleeces was blinding. Rhoda began wandering about and found that low trees and hedges in the fields had wisps of gold festooning them, where the sheep had pushed against them. She had only to gather this wool without approaching the terrifying beasts at all. She went on wandering till she had a glorious armful of soft, glowing fluff.

With this she returned to the rock-hewn sanctuary and found a large room with a table set for a meal. She had eaten nothing since morning and the afternoon was wearing on, so she was pleased to see that such thought had been taken for her needs. She placed the pile of raw wool on a chest and sat down to enjoy her meal. She was waited on by a little dwarf in green, who was just as unable to converse with her as the boatman had been who brought her to the island. When she finished he removed everything from the table and went out. Left alone she stood up and looked around. She then noticed a beautiful wooden spinning wheel. She had never spun, but it seemed clear that this was intended for spinning the gold fleece into yarn.

There didn't seem much she could do about it, but she

remembered the woman who had entered the dull dining room where she was feasting with her family who had made wonders seem possible, and the towering figure which had appeared over the sea by moonlight. Suddenly, she found herself sitting down at the wheel, taking the wool and finding that her fingers seemed to know how to manage the mechanism with its alarmingly sharp spindle. The wheel whirred at speed and a length of sparkling gold thread began to appear. It was as though she was possessed by a spinner of yarn in two senses, because as Rhoda saw and handled the wool from the ferocious sheep, wonderful fantasies passed through her mind in abundance and held her interest as the hours wore on. At length all the raw wool was spun and a great tiredness overwhelmed her. She looked around and saw a bed made of a few covers and a pillow on a large settle. She lay down and fell asleep immediately.

Rhoda had no watch, but it seemed like the very wee small hours when she woke up to see moonlight streaming in at a window. A wind had sprung up and was moaning and wailing around. Suddenly her eyes fell on a large flagon next to the settle on which she lay, standing on a small table of its own. The pale light showed it up against the dark surroundings. It gleamed with a wonderful, nacreous sheen of opaque white glass which appeared like mother-of-pearl. She was sure it had not been there when she went to sleep. How had it arrived in the meantime? Rhoda felt so wide awake and curious that she arose and went to the window. It looked another way from the stream and meadows she had explored the day before. The moon was full and against its light she saw high, rocky mountains, making dark, jagged shapes. Then she saw a torrent of water coming from a source high in the rocks. It gleamed bright silver with reflected moonlight. Gazing at it, she felt a pull, less of attraction than of dread, as though an inexorable thread of fate drew her towards it.

It did not seem advisable to go mountaineering by moonlight, so she returned to her place of rest and tried to sleep. This was not easy, especially as the wind increased and sometimes threw a sharp shower against the window. When daylight came, it was dimmed by low cloud and neither sun nor moon could be seen. The strange glass flagon had lost its lustre and appeared a dull white. She found that a leather thong was attached round it, so that she could wear it around her neck while leaving her hands free. She did not see the dwarf who had waited on her at supper, but a small meal had been laid out for her. When she had eaten it, she took up the vessel and went to look for a door facing in the right northerly direction. She found an opening without seeing anyone. Rocky steps led down from it and she scrambled down, taking care that the precious flagon round her neck did not swing against a hard surface. The mountains seemed more distant than when she had seen them from the window, and as she walked towards them over rough terrain she feared she would be exhausted before her task even began.

Rhoda did not doubt that her third labour was to fill the bottle with water from the inaccessible torrent, but if the first two had seemed hard, this appeared positively life-threatening. The first romance of her adventure had worn off and she began to remember the holiday with her father and sisters, which had seemed so tame and tedious, with some regret. She wondered whether they were alarmed at her absence, and whether she could ever be reached again on this mysterious island, if she did not find her way back.

As she approached the sheer cliffs ahead, the ground was increasingly rock-strewn and it was easy to stumble or twist her ankle. At times squally showers beat in her face on a cold northerly wind, delaying her progress and soaking her clothes. Soon, however, all sound of wind and rain was drowned in the increasing roar of the tremendous cataract. She found as she approached, that it was surrounded by slippery rocks.

As she gazed, she was horrified to see huge snakes slithering among them and rearing venomous heads in a threatening manner.

She stood still, wondering what on Earth she was doing there, and then, above all the other tumultuous sounds, she heard the whirr of mighty wings. Fearing more danger, she looked up at once and was astounded to see a tremendous bird above her, with a noble, eagle-like head and a wing-span that seemed to fill the sky. The huge beak opened and a great voice emerged, authoritative, but gentle.

'Give me your bottle, little girl,' it said. 'You cannot go any further.'

'Thank you, sir,' gasped Rhoda in amazement. She took the flagon fumblingly from her neck and held it up as high as she could reach above her head. The bird hovered above and seized the leather thong in its beak, then circled the raging, foaming waters and dipped the vessel, filling it to the brim. Its flight was so beautiful, Rhoda willed the moment of its return to be indefinitely prolonged. As the great wings plunged down the precipice towards her, she marvelled at the rows of mighty pinions, making their owner free of the wide air. She grabbed the bottle as it swung towards her from the sharp eagle beak.

'Oh, I'm so grateful! You've saved my life,' she called. Her voice seemed to be swept away by the wind and water, but the bird had heard.

'Courage, Rhoda,' it called and turned at once, wheeling clear of the cliffs and becoming distant, high and small in an incredibly short time.

'I still need it,' she thought, fastening the now heavier vessel around her neck and turning to go back over the slippery rocks, fearing for its safety every moment. As she approached the rocky stronghold, the weather became even more tempestuous. Though it was near midday, thick clouds admitted little light from the sun. Suddenly she noticed a small figure emerge from a door and come towards her. She was delighted to recognise the flute player she had encountered the day before. He came up to her and called over the blast of the wind.

'Everything is changed by the accomplishment of your three tasks. It is dangerous to stay another moment. We must take the boat and flee. Follow me.'

Rhoda was startled and stood still. She did not want to abandon the enchanted island. The wonderful lady had invited her and put the tasks before her. Where was she now? She thought the boy's approach rather bossy. He was rushing off without even looking back at her. As she stood wondering, there was a fearful roaring sound and the Earth under her feet began to tremble. She realised there was no time for thought, and clutching the precious bottle with its hard-won contents, she followed the boy as fast as she could. Without re-entering the castle, he found an entrance to the cavern where the little boat had been fastened by the dwarf and they reached it by another route. No dwarf sailor men were to be seen now in the dim light. Without a word the boy helped her into the vessel and cast off, rowing for the opening of the cave. When they got out of the sheltered area, mountainous seas confronted them.

'Pour a little water from your bottle into the sea,' the boy commanded.

'Will it help?' she asked, amazed.

'Try.'

She tipped up the beautiful flagon, letting a single precious drop fall into the deep, boiling sea and disappear. It seemed wasteful and futile, but where it had dropped, the sea became flat and the violence of the waves was suppressed. The boy hoisted the sail and the wind bore the boat on an even course, though further from them it still blew with hurricane force.

In a very short time they caught sight of the coast where Rhoda and her family had been having their holiday. She was anything but pleased to see it. She was enjoying being in the little boat with the boy who seemed to be omniscient and so concerned for her. She had a feeling her family's attitude on this occasion might be very different. The boat blew in at the harbour without seeming to need steering and the boy lowered the sails as it came to the jetty. It was still stormy with howling wind and driving rain and the place was deserted.

'Be careful of your bottle,' said the boy. 'Remember, a drop from it will still any kind of storm.'

'Aren't you coming with me?' asked Rhoda in dismay, feeling cold and gloomy. He only smiled and shook his head, as he handed her out of the boat and turned it around. Soon the sails were up and he was tacking away without much difficulty, in the teeth of the on-shore wind. Rhoda had to find the steep path leading up the cliff by herself. The bottle seemed suddenly heavier. She held on to a protruding root and looked out to sea. Already the little boat was only a speck in which the figure of her guide was no longer visible.

When Rhoda reached the top she saw three buffeted shapes in

mackintoshes, leaning into the wind and coming towards her. Then one of them looked up and saw her, gave a shout and stood still. At this the tallest straightened and she saw it was her father. He streaked across the remaining distance and had her in his arms.

'Rhoda!' Mavis was not far behind him. 'Where've you been?' she asked in a fury born of prolonged anxiety.

'I went in the lady's boat,' Rhoda began. The atmosphere seemed all wrong for giving her stupendous adventure the right impact.

'I said so,' said Myrtle sarcastically. 'Enjoying herself without us as usual and ruining our holiday.'

'Whatever's the thing round your neck?' asked Mavis. Rhoda took the strap off without a word and held up the bottle. She tipped it slowly and let one drop of water slip over the brim and fall among them. Suddenly the wind moderated and a ray of light escaped through a gap in the clouds, illuminating the falling rain drops. She felt Father and Mavis relax and her own calm return.

'I'm sorry I had to go without you. I'll tell you the whole story,' said Rhoda.

'We had a fright,' said her father. 'It's good to have you back.' Rhoda was pleased to be among them. Her story could be shared and relived. One day they would all visit that island together.

THE RAINBOW PLANET

— ✦ —

The sitting room was dark. All eyes were focused intently on a television screen. Rhoda and her family were passing a winter evening with a video lent by a friend, showing what purported to be life on a hitherto unknown planet whose position in the universe was not disclosed. So engrossed were the watchers that their bodily surroundings and positions were completely forgotten. The planet was first shown from afar, as though seen from an approaching spaceship. In the dark of space it appeared as a sphere of rainbow light. At the top was pure white, then a band of yellow. Next came orange and red. The colours then continued in the order of the spectrum, with violet, blue, green, then again yellow, orange and a red belt, dominating the other colours and encircling the planet's equator. In the southern hemisphere, the bands of colour followed the same order in reverse, from red to red and then orange, yellow and finally white at the south pole.

Now the camera showed the surface in the green band of light. There were streams of water everywhere, and little waterfalls, so that the sound of refreshing wetness never ceased.

There was greenness in the air and sky and the rocks and stones were green in themselves without the help of lichen or algae.

They seemed to contain crystalline elements, because they

caught the light, which also sparkled from water drops as the streams swirled round them. Even clouds and sunlight had a green quality, as when they are seen on Earth through coloured cellophane paper, or tinted spectacles. The camera picked out small frogs, snails, or similar amphibians and molluscs and insects like grasshoppers, all in every conceivable different shade of green, with patterns of greenish yellow or grey.

Such was the quality of concentration of Rhoda and her family, that they seemed actually to be in the picture, moving of their own free will. There were no sounds of mechanical things, like aeroplanes or traffic, however distant. The air was pure and refreshing and the whole landscape clean. As Rhoda stood, marvelling at all this, she had the impression that someone was looking at her from behind. Turning round, she saw nothing but a group of trees, of different species. There was a huge, gnarled one in the centre, which reached up an immense height into the sky, some of more moderate height, and some small and dainty. One of these appeared to wobble strangely in the wind, though looking round at the others she saw no movement among their leaves and could not feel much breeze on her face. A further stir of the young sapling caught her attention, and then she could have no more doubt of it; the tree was moving in relation to the ground, of its own volition, skipping gracefully and whirling in pirouettes. Astounded, Rhoda whispered to her family to look behind. As her father and sisters turned round, they gasped. More of the trees were demonstrating mobility.

With great dignity, in movements exactly suited to their particular shape and formation, the trees of many kinds danced in and out in ever different formations. Rhoda and her family seemed to hear a kind of music, composed of water and wind-like sounds, melodious and soberly cheerful, expressive of the primeval energy of all green things. Suddenly, among the waving boughs, heavenly bodies could be seen in motion, as though participating in the grand measure. Rhoda saw first a red one, like our sun in a very misty sunrise on Earth, then an orange, a yellow, a green, a blue and a violet, slowly following each other and visible in spite of the greenish daylight still illuminating everything.

'What are those, Dad?' asked Myrtle.

'They must be moons. This planet has six moons, one for each colour of the rainbow,' said their father in wonder. As they gazed into the beautiful tracery of leaves and branches over their heads, they saw many varieties of birds which appeared caught up in ecstasy, dancing with their feet on the branches and balancing themselves with outstretched wings.

Rhoda was watching passively, though intently absorbed. Suddenly, she felt her whole body tremble, as though charged with an excess of energy. Then she was away, without knowing what steps to take, or having any conscious volition. She belonged with the scene, and moved among the trees as one of them. Without fatigue, and as if partially liberated from the force of gravity, she sailed up and descended gracefully. She no longer saw her family and concluded that they must have come to in the sitting room at home and be passing round snacks. She was thus the only human dancing in Paradise, until she suddenly caught sight of the couple. Among the waving branches of celebrating trees, figures appeared, human in shape, dazzling to look on. They wore, not cloth but light, their flesh like mother-of-pearl, glowing white, around them circles of colour like the bands on the Rainbow Planet itself. Their movements expressed harmony with each other and their surroundings.

Suddenly there was darkness. Rhoda's body had resumed its usual weighted feeling and she found herself sitting in her ordinary chair at home. A sisterly elbow gave her a great nudge and a most terrestrial plate of biscuits was presented to her.

On the screen before them, images of waving branches still suggested Paradise, but it had become another world.

'This is a very long video,' said Myrtle in a complaining voice, and she wriggled and yawned hugely.

'You're tired, dear,' said Dad. 'It's about time all you little girls were in bed.' This disgusting piece of flagrant parental tyranny was greeted with the howls of indignation it deserved, but at that moment the attention of father and daughters alike was distracted by a strange phenomenon. A whirring sound, not loud but totally alien and subtly threatening, fell on their ears. Curious prickling sensations entered their bodies, as of mild electrical currents. Terror gripped and paralysed them. The door opened and something entered, vaguely human in form, but robot-like in appearance and motion. There was no common language, but they knew without words, or looking at each other, that they were dominated by irresistible power. They rose up out of their chairs, as one human, and followed the towering metallic figure out of the front door into the dark garden, where something in the way of a vehicle was standing.

A dim red light emanated from it. It was round, without windows, or a back or a front. No wheels were visible beneath it, but it seemed slightly raised above ground level. There was no door or way in, yet they found themselves drawn towards it and lifted as though weightless till they passed through the walls, which were not solid. They experienced an intensification of the electric tingling in their bodies, and of red light around them as they passed inside.

The looming figure followed them in and the whirring in their ears increased as they suddenly left the garden and seemed instantly to be away out in space, without any of the jolts or rocketings which a terrestrial spaceship would have required to leave the Earth. They had scarcely time to notice their own reactions or whether they were standing or supported on anything, before the dim red around them seemed to glow much more brightly. Their vehicle stopped abruptly, but without a bump. The metallic figure led the way through the wall, and they were impelled to follow. They were in a red world. Rhoda was reminded of the green sky and surroundings of the Paradise they had lately left through want of concentration, but here were no flowing water or plant forms. They were on a huge plain strewn with boulders, both ground and rocks a brownish red. In the distance they saw mountains, volcanic cones ridiculously steep and pointed. Beside them was a large building which appeared to be made of something like concrete.

It had neither doors nor windows, but they soon found themselves inside and were surrounded by every conceivable kind of machinery, all whirring and vibrating. No noise was very loud in itself, but the total effect was disturbing and stressful. The prickly feelings they had had since the invasion of the sitting room at home by the alien entity and which had not ceased on the journey, were now much in evidence. Looking round, they realised that many other such non-human and robot-like figures were operating all the computers and other gear. There were screens showing strange signs and shapes which they could not interpret. Nothing interfered with their freedom of movement and they finally made bold to wander about, like visitors to an exhibition, but keeping together and looking around in case of unexpected attack. At last they found a screen which showed the whole of the Rainbow Planet with its bands of bright colour, like the picture in the video they had watched at home. The scene narrowed as they gazed to the red band in the middle of the northern hemisphere, then went southwards, showing violet and blue bands, and finally the green which they recognised as the Paradise they had lately explored.

The very sight of it was cheering and they began to relax a little, but then were horrified to see what appeared to be an invasion of red robots infiltrating the green world. The picture concentrated on a strip of green forest bordering the blue band which they could now see was water, a girdle of blue ocean circling the planet. The red shapes teemed upon the shore, apparently streaming out of a submersible craft of some sort. As they advanced upon the green world, everything began to dry up. The green turned yellowish, then brown. Streams faltered and failed to flow. Then there was a stir from further within the green area where forests began. The trees were becoming mobile and advancing in a terrifying manner. As well as seeing the picture on screen, the watchers could hear a roar as of a gale among branches. The trees in a dense phalanx bore down upon the invaders. When they came within the influence of whatever was causing desertification, they trembled and some of their branches curled up, withered and fell off. In spite of this, they seized up robots as soon as they could reach them and pressed them in a deadly embrace. Great tremors, as of anguish, wracked the trees as they came into the field of the electrical radiation from which Rhoda and her family had suffered since entering the red world, but they persisted in a boa-like action of squeezing their prey. The robots became limp and ineffective under this treatment and could be hurled back into the sea.

Without knowing how she had arrived there, Rhoda found herself in bed. She seemed to have slept, but still felt an overwhelming fatigue. She remembered the family journey to the Rainbow Planet in the alarming company of the wordless, sinister figure. She shuddered to think of the battle on the border of the green temperate zone in the northern hemisphere, but recalled that the power of the paradisal trees appeared to be invincible. She lay and listened in the silent house. Her sisters, who shared her room, were breathing evenly in a way indicating peaceful sleep. From his room down the passage, Dad's snores could be heard reverberating intermittently in a way she usually thought disturbing, but now found comfortingly homely after their outlandish and exhausting experiences. Then deep sleep descended over her, but this time she dreamt vividly. She was wandering all alone in the green world, over grass and rocks, crossing streams by stepping stones, thinking of the couple she had glimpsed so briefly at the peak of the dance she and her family had witnessed in their first visit, wishing she could find them. Then she began seeing strange faces. In the bark of trees, or on stones with mossy patches, she noticed ill-assorted eyes, mouths, noses. It was all imagination, but once she started to see them, she could see nothing else in the natural forms around her. Gradually, the impression accumulated that she was being watched and that all was no longer quite wholesome and harmless in Paradise.

As she went on, Rhoda found the ground was rising and becoming less fertile, like terrestrial moorland. It was cooler and breezier and the few trees were twisted as though they had had gales to contend with from infancy. They no longer struck her as gay and friendly, but rather grotesque and even threatening in appearance. There was a springy plant under foot like heather which was pleasant to walk through, but she had to watch out for half-hidden stones and rocks which could trip her up. At length the ground seemed to be levelling off in a sort of plateau. There was a large area of quite short green stuff like grass on Earth. Then she saw the standing stones. They were amazingly tall and slender, and at first she had the impression of a group of enormous human figures petrified in movement. She felt somewhat alarmed but drawn nevertheless to investigate. If the rocks in general and other things had seemed to have strange faces since the beginning of her dream journey, coming among these stones was just like meeting a group of people. They were arranged in an approximate circle with a fairly even gradation in height from one side to the other. Rhoda walked rather nervously to the centre of the ring and had the impression of being observed from all round.

The stones were not so much like a prehistoric monument on Earth, thousands of years old and deeply embedded in the turf, as like something mobile and recently arrived. As Rhoda looked at their bases, they appeared to her poised rather than fixed. She stared in wonder, then saw with consternation that the area underneath them was becoming blurred, as though mist swirled round it. Then it was obvious that there was a gap between stone and soil, no longer wreathed in vapour, or shimmering with energy, but quite clear. There she was in the middle of a lot of heavy, unpredictable moving bodies. They could close in and crush her if the circle broke, but it seemed rather as though a great round dance was in progress. The ring remained as large as when it was on the ground and fairly evenly spaced, but the stones were moving in a surprisingly nimble and graceful way, considering their mass and probable weight. The effect of all this on Rhoda was not like the ecstasy of her first visit to the Rainbow Planet. The stony dancers remained alien to her and she had no urge to take part. She felt sad and apprehensive rather than elated, though there was fascination in watching such an eerie spectacle.

Finally the tallest stone of all approached Rhoda in her central position at an unthreatening, stately pace, and halted a few yards in front of her. She gazed at it and saw indistinctly the figure and face of a wise-looking ancient sage. The eyes were deep hollows in the surface, dark and damp. Without having pupils or irises, they nonetheless seemed to fix her with a penetrating gaze. A nose was suggested by a few lines and scratches at the right distance beneath the apparent eye sockets and below this a deep, crooked gash could be seen as a mouth. As with the alien who had carried her family off in a spaceship, Rhoda did not think there could be any common language between a human and the petrine apparition which now confronted her, yet she distinctly heard in her mind, rather than from the unlikely maw, comprehensible speech.

'What are you looking for?' it asked.

'The man and woman who live here,' she answered.

'My own destination exactly. Let us go together.'

'Who are you? asked Rhoda.

'In my own country I was known as the Inventor.'

'Which country is that?'

'Unfortunately the ocean wave has covered it deep for centuries past, but we ourselves knew how to survive.'

'How can you move when you are so big and heavy?' she asked.

'My people are the conquerors of matter. The greater the density and mass, the greater the release of electro-magnetic energy for propulsion. We can dematerialise, disappear at will, move with the speed of thought to any destination.'

'Could you take me with you?' asked Rhoda. This was the end of the conversation in the moor-like area among the stones. As soon as this rash suggestion was uttered, she began to feel very queer indeed. It was worse than a faint, because she just wasn't there any more, and neither was anything around or under her. Luckily, this uncanny phase was momentary. After it she felt her body as solid as ever, as though it had just been given back to her. She was in a warmer, brighter place full of greenness. She looked around for the stone sage who had presumably transported her by technology superior to that of Earth. Ahead of her she saw an immense tree whose roots formed a cave-like shelter with natural seats within it. On one of these was a figure, white and gleaming. Rhoda at once recognised the woman she had seen earlier on her former visit to the Rainbow Planet, when the trees had danced. She wondered how to approach and whether they would have a language in common, when she noticed something else. The woman held a pipe or flute to her mouth and was playing upon it. In front of her, swaying in response to the tune, was a huge snake.

The woman and the snake were too absorbed to notice Rhoda, who came quite close to them and sat among the tree roots. Presently the woman stopped playing and laid her instrument down. The snake curled up in front of her, rearing its head, on a level with her face, and then Rhoda overheard a conversation.

'You must be horribly bored here with nothing to do,' began the snake, with something that looked like a yawn. The woman looked surprised.

'What is "bored"?' she asked.

'There's just nothing here except the countryside,' answered the serpent in disgust. 'No towns, no people, no one to govern or control.'

'You're wrong, friend,' she replied. 'Everything is here. I am mother in this world. Every leaf and petal and creature, every stone and pool is whole, full of energy, a centre of love. Life is going on here, full of purpose. The trees, the hills, the rivers interconnect with us, my husband and I, and we are at the very heart of them all.'

'It's very pious of you, dear lady, to be contented with your lot,' said the serpent, 'but what can you actually do or become? Can you, yourself, create anything new?'

'Everything is new, serpent. I create when I look. The light from me comes back, reflected from all the life which surrounds us. Matter is radiating and vibrating. It is creative just to be in this holy place. You must be careful how and what you think here, creature. Paradise will reject what is out of harmony with the whole.'

'It's wonderful to hear you, mother of all,' said the snake, 'but you will do well to listen to me. I am older than you are. I've had experiences you've never dreamt of. There are worlds beyond your green garden of this planet of yours alone, and beyond is the infinity of space.'

Rhoda was thrilled by the lady's words and wanted always to remember them. At the same time, she was furious with the serpent's contemptuous reception of such precious revelations. She felt she must have overheard this conversation for a purpose, and could no longer sit unnoticed while an enemy of Paradise tried to pervert the mind of its inhabitant. She stood and moved towards them.

'Snake,' she said, 'if what you say is true, take me to your own place and then let me return to tell the mistress of Paradise if it is so much more exciting than the quiet existence of nature.'

'Who is this?' asked the lady in surprise. 'Where do you come from?'

'I come from another planet called Earth,' Rhoda said.

'What is it like?' asked the lady.

'It's very good, but gravely imperilled,' Rhoda answered. 'There are millions and millions of humans, not just two, and the way they live is altering the atmosphere and the climate. It may not be sustainable.'

'These are big words for a little girl,' the serpent interrupted them derisively. 'No doubt you are repeating what they tell you in school. I know far more. Earth is my planet and I can take you back in time to a culture long forgotten.'

Suddenly there was a green flash and Rhoda saw something streak towards a dark opening under the tree. The head had already disappeared into it and was followed by more and more gleaming green scales. At last a pointed tail reared up and Rhoda darted forward to grab it before she lost the chance.

'Take care, little girl,' the lady called in alarm.

'I'll come back,' said Rhoda, rather breathlessly, but with a brave smile. She carefully memorised her last glimpse of the shining, loving woman, as she found the dark hole close around her.

The tunnel continued for miles but their speed was terrific. Air whizzed past Rhoda's ears, becoming fresher and beginning to smell of the sea. Finally they emerged into a cave on the coast where there was deep water in front of them. A strange craft floated upon it and the snake contracted in length to the height or a tall man. It acquired arms and legs with amazing rapidity and a head which retained a rather snakelike, greenish appearance but carried a kingly crown.

'Come with me, dear little girl,' he said with authority, opening a door in the side of the vehicle. He stepped in, keeping his balance with dignity as it bobbed about and reached toward Rhoda to assist her to step off the rock on which she was standing. There seemed no alternative for her but to join him at whatever risk. As soon as they were inside, the great cylindrical object sped away from the coast and soon became airborne. Noise and speed increased and it did not seem long till they saw a blue planet before them, becoming bigger and showing a distinction between seas and continents. Finally they were above a great ocean and losing height. Then Rhoda saw land, a vast island covered with walls and towers and waving palm trees.

'What is this?' asked Rhoda.

'Mine, all mine, every inch of it,' replied the king, bursting with pride. They came to land on an open space which seemed to be in the middle of great buildings. Hundreds of figures ran towards their spacecraft the moment it touched down. The king alighted first and all his subjects flattened themselves on their faces, apparently in awe and terror. He turned back to Rhoda and said, 'Welcome to Superworld! Never has there been such a well-run kingdom as this. My control is absolute, as you see. I know what every one of these people is thinking. Everything in their minds comes from me.'

Rhoda thought she was in for a dull time, but not knowing how to drive the spaceship and take off alone, she had no alternative but to alight as calmly as she could. The king clapped his hands and everyone stood up instantly. The impression they gave Rhoda was one of unrelieved greyness. They wore grey trousers and jackets of a light, synthetic material and all had grey hair and even greyish skin on their hands and faces. As she looked at those nearest her, it seemed as though they were all clones of the same individual. It was the same face everywhere, with regular, undistinguished features and the same expression, or lack of one.

'Hospitality group, come here,' ordered the king. Half a dozen figures advanced. 'This young lady is our guest,' he continued. 'Take her to her quarters and see to her needs.' They surrounded Rhoda and began to march. She was obliged to go with them and felt more like a prisoner than a guest. They crossed the huge courtyard in the hot sun and came at last to the high wall on one side. A door swung open at their approach and they all passed through. The walls inside were of undressed stone in huge blocks. It was difficult to imagine how the builders could have manipulated them into position. Opposite the door was a staircase of stone leading to a higher level. Rhoda's escort moved her towards this and went up with and around her. A door at the stair head led into a chamber with windows looking out onto the space where the king's spaceship had landed and also in the opposite direction, where there was a garden of palm trees and tropical flowers and fruits.

The ceiling was high and the floor of flagstones smoother than the stone walls, with coloured, patterned rugs strewn in places. There was a low bed with a woven coverlet and a few wooden chairs with bright cushions. A table by the bedhead had water in a glass flagon, a china drinking bowl and an attractive arrangement of tropical fruits in a beautiful wooden vessel shaped like a ship. Rhoda stepped in and looked around her. Then she turned back towards the door and found that all the people who had brought her had already disappeared. She tried the door and discovered that it was locked. Disconcerted, she went to a chair and sat, looking towards the space where she had landed.

All the architecture in this land was massive. She saw a huge structure of hewn blocks of stone in a platform which had a smaller one on top of it. Above those was a third and on that, outlined against the sky, one great slab suggested an altar. Presently she noticed some of the grey figures of the inhabitants coming and going in long robes. She thought they might be preparing for some ceremony. She felt suddenly depressed and very weary. She turned back to the room and found the water and fruit more inviting than the external scene. It was cooler in the stone building than outside, but still warm and close, as though thunder might be in the offing. She found the water refreshing and the fruits delicious.

As no one appeared to require anything of her, she lay down on the bed and turned to look at the window away from the altar structure. The sight of the garden was soothing and reminded her of Paradise and the lady for whose sake she had risked this journey. With these cheering memories, she drifted off to sleep. When she woke up the light was different and strange blasts were coming from some sort of horn or trumpet. Moonlight flooded the room from the courtyard side. She got up and went to look out. The priests were whirling now in what appeared to be mounting frenzy. They threw their arms skywards and uttered bloodcurdling ululations. On the top of the stone platform, Rhoda could see a dominating figure whom she suspected was the king, outlined against the moon and apparently issuing commands. Suddenly her silent quarters were echoing to many footsteps and the door burst open. Those who entered, though more animated than those she had seen by day when she arrived, seemed all the less human. Their exuberance appeared more drug-induced than natural. Their eyes rolled as they surrounded her in a sort of dance and obliged her to go with them without words.

When they emerged into the open, they wove to and fro, leading Rhoda around in narrowing circles, till they came close to the structure which seemed awaiting a sacrificial victim. They mounted the three platforms, circling round each one before resuming the ascent. When she came out on the top, the king loomed silently against the night sky, no longer the suave and amusing host, but a figure dominated from within by an irresistible and fatal force. He and his minions were screaming in their barbaric language and at a malign gesture towards Rhoda, those around seized and bound her and laid her upon the great altar slab. The air was hot and full of electricity. Thunder growled out at sea, but the sky above remained clear. Rhoda looked up and saw a huge, brilliant planet hanging serenely over her.

The king unsheathed a cruel knife with a long, sickle-shaped blade which caught the light of the declining full moon in the west. He brandished it above the helpless victim on the altar in readiness for the kill, but the planet was too quick for him.

It sped Earthwards and became a towering female figure of light. Every being on the scene fell down in a dead faint at sight of her, except the king, who froze, as though turned to stone, the knife still held aloft over his head. The planet lady was followed by her son, a boy a little older than Rhoda. Dressed as an astronaut, he sprang up the steps to the altar, produced a knife and cut her bonds in a moment. Rhoda sat up and gazed at him in gratitude and wonder, but was not given much time to absorb this further abrupt change in her fortunes from death to life.

'Come with me to the spaceship before this lot wake up again,' the boy said urgently. The craft which the king had arrived in still stood where he had landed with Rhoda, and the boy led her across to it. The lady towered, brilliant, over the scene, shedding as much light as had the full moon, now set. By this radiance they boarded the craft. The boy sat at the controls while Rhoda got in beside him. It took off without the noise and commotion of a modern terrestrial space rocket, or even a jet plane, and it was soon way above the Earth, which appeared round and blue, as when Rhoda had first seen it on arrival from space.

'Where are we going?' asked Rhoda.

'Back to Paradise on the Rainbow Planet,' the pilot answered. 'The lady there is very anxious to see you safe again.'

It did not seem long before the planet with its bands of six colours appeared before them, growing fast as they approached with a speed vastly greater than that of a terrestrial spaceship.

The pilot made for the green band in the upper hemisphere and came to land on an open space in the warm, fertile, open area where Rhoda and her family had first arrived. The boy jumped down and helped Rhoda out. Together they advanced through the sweet air, perfumed by innumerable kinds of flowering tree and shrub. As they went, they saw another couple approaching from among huge trees at the side of the open space. Rhoda recognised the lady she had last seen talking to the serpent and the man she had glimpsed as her partner in the dance of the trees and moons. As they met, the lady sprang to embrace her.

'What happened to you? Where is that snake I talked with?' she asked. 'Did he take you to a wonderful kingdom?'

'They had her all trussed up on a stone slab,' said the boy. 'The wicked old rascal was standing over her with a knife when I got there with my mother.'

'How appalling!' the lady exclaimed. 'You must come away and rest and drink some restorative cordial.'

Then Rhoda enjoyed rest and refreshment in the company of people she loved and never wanted to leave. The boy explained that what had happened to Rhoda on her journey back in time and space had made Paradise on the Rainbow Planet forever secure against the attempts of its enemies to overrun and pollute it. In the end, exhaustion crept up on her and she was laid on a bed of moss and leaves where she fell into a deep sleep.

When she awoke, feeling strong and joyful, she found that she was in the glade with the shining couple no longer. She was back in the house in the sisters' bedroom. This was a jolt, but she knew she also belonged on the distant planet shown in the video. Even when they could not sit down and watch, she could recall all the scenes she had passed through, as they were now part of herself.

Part Two
— ❧ —

CHAPTER ONE

Myth and Tale

— ❧ —

The myth of Cupid and Psyche is traditionally interpreted as describing experiences of a soul in search of reality and fulfilment. It is not part of the corpus of ancient Greek myth, but was written in the second century AD with a deliberately allegorical intention. At this date, outside Christian circles, polytheism was still credible, though it had reached a late and decadent stage. 'Cupid and Psyche' had a profound and lasting appeal and was taken into Christian culture. In medieval and modern Europe, however, gods and goddesses had to be dropped, and the myth gave rise to a series of folktale derivatives, of which the one best known as Beauty and the Beast is the closest to the original. The myth gives Psyche two elder sisters, who presumably stand for elements in human beings which war against their spiritual progress and must therefore be ruthlessly discarded and destroyed, as the myth says the god brings about their death. In folktales they become a couple of largely undifferentiated female villains, heading for disaster. This motif of the three sisters, of which only the youngest is wise and successful, while the two older ones try spitefully to ruin her happiness, is very widespread in folktale and frequently occurs in stories not obviously connected with Cupid and Psyche, such as Cinderella, or the source Shakespeare used for *King Lear*.

Cupid and Psyche is an archetypal story of great power and complexity, which is used to striking effect in CS Lewis's mature novel *Till We Have Faces*. A master in the great world of myth and story, as well as a Christian apologist of rare distinction, Lewis perceives the sisters not just as foils for the perfect Psyche's pathetic appeal, but as crucial elements in the human make-up, and ones which are closer than their sister to the ordinary experience of most of us. In the original myth, a king and queen, who are given no special character or attributes, have three daughters. The two elder are good looking, but the beauty of the youngest is such as to rival that of goddesses.

People spontaneously worship her as she passes, and the cult of Venus, or Aphrodite, is neglected in her favour.

The word 'psyche' in its oldest use, means 'butterfly'. This creature, beautiful and powerful in flight, was regarded as symbolic of the human soul. In Greek thought there was strong dualism in which body and soul were seen as enemies and competitors. The aspiring soul had to fly above the degraded physical, Earthly level of being to achieve virtue and union with the divine. The amazing appearance of Psyche in the story signifies the potential of a purified soul to reach the level of gods and goddesses, or even to surpass them. The myth continues with the two older sisters finding their husbands in neighbouring princes, while no man is found who has the temerity to marry Psyche. As in any perplexity in a Greek story, the king and queen consult the oracle of Apollo. The result is not reassuring. They are told their youngest daughter cannot have a mortal spouse. Her destiny is to be the 'bride of a monster whom neither gods nor men can resist'. This really indicates Cupid, or Eros, who, in this myth stands for the soul's divine lover, but is understood by its recipients to mean that Psyche must be exposed on a mountain for a real Dragon to devour.

When this is done, and the king and his retinue have left, the maiden is quite alone. Eros causes her to be carried by Zephyr to a sacred spot where there are trees and water and a palace of fabulous magnificence, like the abode of a god. This place of endless delights and instruction where all Psyche's needs are anticipated and met, is simply the inner world of all human beings where they can, if they will, encounter God and learn how to live in accord with Him.

Besides Beauty and the Beast, this motif recurs in numerous traditional tales. In dreams, too, our great inner world is often symbolised by a large house, institution, department store or castle, in which it is possible to wander for hours, without reaching the end, or exhausting its resources.

In the myth, the monster is only a rumour, but in folktales it becomes a reality. In King Crin, the prince is under an enchantment, which makes him a pig by day, and another story makes him a serpent, who also goes through a further phase as a bird. In Bellinda and the Monster, his form and appearance are too horrific to describe. It is only said that they could turn the observer to ashes. In the myth, Psyche is, in effect, a human sacrifice, offered up to save other humans from the anger of Aphrodite. In this, it recalls the older stories of Iphigenia at Aulis and Andromeda chained to a rock on the sea coast, to be devoured by an aquatic monster. In The Serpent King, the first and second of three wives are killed by the serpent, because they are base born, but a third is spared because she is a princess. In King Crin, the first and second of three sisters recoil from the pig, who comes in covered in mud, while the third greets him with affection. In Bellinda and the Monster, she has to agree to marry him while he is still hideous, so that he can then appear as the handsome prince he really is.

In fact, divine love and vocation do appear monstrous at the level of worldly wisdom, disrupting relationships and causing bitter separations and misunderstandings. In *Till We Have Faces*, Orual, the older of Psyche's two sisters, is a mother substitute to her and has a tremendously possessive affection. She bitterly resents Psyche's mysterious, apparently inhuman, vocation, and unwittingly becomes herself the heaviest of the many trials of her beloved younger sister. Lewis has made his version a historical novel, set in the period which gives rise to the myth. It is also possible to retell the folktale Bellinda and the Monster in a contemporary, or at least more modern setting than the original, to show that it describes something still going on within and among ourselves in the twenty-first century.

In the original myth, Eros is sent by the wrathful Aphrodite to punish Psyche by making her love some unworthy object, but when he sees her, he is astounded by her beauty and subsequently becomes her protector. All is well while Psyche remains in her palace, alone by day and joined by her divine lover at night. Neither the jealous divine mother-in-law nor her sisters can shatter her joy of their own accord, but Psyche cannot remain content without human companions and she herself asks the god to bring them on a visit. They are given regal hospitality, feasted and fêted, and yet they use the opportunity to sow doubts in their sister's mind about what sort of a being really comes at night in pitch darkness. They still think in terms of the 'monster' to whom Psyche was supposed to be offered up on the mountain. They persuade her to hide a light under a cloak to shine on the nocturnal visitor in his sleep and to have a knife ready to slay the 'monster', if such it is.

Psyche complies with all this. The beauty of Eros asleep beside her is so astounding that she trembles and spills hot oil from her lamp upon him. At this he wakes and at once fate is empowered to bring about what appear at the time to be tragedy and disaster. Eros is compelled to abandon Psyche for the present, so that she is at the mercy of his mother. She wanders in a lonely and terrible exile and Aphrodite lays on her impossible labours which can only be performed with supernatural assistance. In fact Psyche was evidently not mature enough to continue her ecstatic existence in the palace of Eros. Her sisters were indispensable tools of fate who set her on the road which leads to permanent and unshakable union with her divine lover. In the myth, Eros is angry with the sisters and soon brings about their death, by throwing them down a precipice. Perhaps Psyche's purgative experiences bring to an end in her those Earthly and materialistic urges which her sisters represent.

In Bellinda and the Monster the sisters have names and continue to play a role throughout the story. Instead of their coming to the palace, Bellinda has to go home to them for their weddings with local men. All the same, Assunta and Carolina are much the same character and lack any redeeming feature to arouse our sympathy. In the denouement, when Bellinda marries the monster turned prince, they are consumed with impotent envy and spiteful rage, as a result of which they are petrified, literally, and become stone statues on either side of the palace front door.

In *Till We Have Faces,* CS Lewis makes the middle sister, whom he calls Redival, a boy-mad girl interested in sex alone. In this she clearly stands for the level of bodily appetites and egoistic demands which must be left behind by the aspiring soul. The oldest sister is not like this at all, being remarkably ugly to look at, but also exceptionally clever. If Redival represents body, and Psyche soul or spirit, Orual perhaps stands for mind, not in the sense of intellectualism, but rather of practical shrewdness and organising power. When the old king dies without a son or son-in-law, she succeeds to the kingdom with unassuming and common-sensical competence right away.

In the myth, the king is given no particular character. It is just stated that he is regretful but resigned to fate when it comes to offering up his youngest daughter on the mountain for a supposed Dragon to devour. In Lewis's novel he becomes a brute who is only too willing to let Psyche suffer in his stead, as he was afraid a king-sacrifice would be demanded of himself by priest and people.

In Bellinda and the Monster, it is the merchant who is the father of the three sisters who comes first upon the enchanted palace while walking in a vast forest. All his needs as a traveller are met by unseen hands and when he sees a rose bush in the grounds there seems no reason why he should not pick one as a present for Bellinda. When he does so, the monster appears in a fury and makes him promise on pain of death to send her to the palace in his stead. When he returns home and tells his daughters about this narrow escape, Bellinda agrees cheerfully to go back to the monster, to save her father and sisters from his vengeance.

By and large, Beauty and the Beast and the other tales in this group, focus upon the first part of the myth, in which the palace of Eros plays a central role. The myth is very much longer than such tales and contains a whole further corpus of events which

65

follow Psych's expulsion from the castle of delight. She is perhaps unique in ancient story in playing what is usually a male role of wandering, striving and suffering. Only one tale in Calvino's Italian collection obviously stems from the episode of the tasks of Aphrodite. This is The Ship with Three Decks. Here, significantly, the role of wanderer and achiever is assumed by a young man, while the woman corresponding to Psyche is a passive prisoner on a remote island somewhere out at sea. There is a very long preamble in which the King of England in a heavy disguise becomes godfather to a poor Italian boy. He tells the parents to send him to be his godfather's heir when he grows up. This happens, but he is dogged by a villain who tries to usurp his adoption by the king.

When he arrives in England, the youth hears of the king's daughter on an island no one knows where. There is a further complicated preamble in which the youth is helped by a wise sailor to win the cooperation of insects, animals and birds, without which he will not be able to save the princess. When he finally arrives at her island, he finds her the prisoner of a mysterious 'Fairy Sabiana', who plainly assumes the role of the malevolent goddess in the myth. He must perform three tasks to release the princess. Two of these are the same as those of Psyche. A pile of mixed grains and pulses must be sorted in a single night. This is accomplished with the help of innumerable ants. Psyche had to obtain the fleeces of fierce, man-eating sheep, but the youth has to remove a mountain. This is done with the help of enough rats to make it a single night's work. Finally, the fairy demands a barrel full of the water of life. This is obtained from a dangerous and inaccessible mountain height by summoning a flock of vultures to whom he has previously done a good turn. This corresponds to the eagle bringing water from the Styx to Psyche.

It is interesting to reflect on the differences between the tale and the original myth, as well as the similarities. The most striking difference is the appearance of the sea and the remote island, not exactly located on any map. The vast complexity and importance of the sea image is worth a chapter of its own.

CHAPTER TWO

The Sea

— ❦ —

The contemporary poet, Geoffrey Hill, in his poem 'Genesis' which forms an impressive opening to his first collection and his whole oeuvre, explores the possibilities and limitations of the sea as meaningful myth. In the first place, it is something which counterbalances and challenges the unimaginative stolidity of dry land:

> Against the burly air I strode
> Crying the miracles of God.
> And first I brought the sea to bear
> Upon the dead weight of the land;

He is not to be beguiled by too romantic a notion. The great, graceful birds which float upon the wild elements of air and sea, the osprey and hawk, are pitiless killers, leaving an edging of red blood along the margin of the waves. Human flesh is analogous to dull clods of Earth and lowly soil and the watery element stands for the transcendence of such mortality.

> And I renounced on the fourth day,
> this fierce and unregenerate clay,

> Building as a huge myth for man
> The watery Leviathan,

Here are introduced, besides the imperfectly visualised aquatic monster, the mythical phoenix and the albatross, real but decked in marvellous legend.

> And made the long-winged albatross
> Sow the ashes of the sea
> Where Capricorn and Zero cross
> A brooding immortality –
> Such as the charmed phoenix has
> In the unwithering tree.

Here again, the tendency to romanticise is a threat to real meaning:

> The phoenix burns as cold as frost;
> And, like a legendary ghost,
> The phantom-bird goes wild and lost,
> Upon a pointless ocean tossed.
> So, on the fifth day, I turned again
> To flesh and blood and the blood's pain.

Images tossed up by the world's poets must have attractive grace and impressive stature, but they are there to help us face our real fears and the many besetting problems in our ordinary lives which often seem trivial and a hindrance to our lofty aspirations. The beautiful creation, so beguiling in its most common naturalness, contains threats of inhuman and unimaginable proportions. Though gifted with the poet's age-old sensitivity to beauty and significance in the world, Geoffrey Hill cannot forget that he writes in the age of the Holocaust and the nuclear bomb. Such threats to positive meaning on a cosmic scale make every individual's petty burdens and annoyances more degrading and depressing.

In his book *Care of the Soul*, the distinguished American contemporary Jungian psychologist, Thomas Moore, writes of the tendency of his patients to come with problems which they expect him to clear out of the way, so that they can conform to an image of social adjustment. He refuses to oblige in this way and insists on looking for a positive meaning in the most unpromising symptoms or circumstances. According to him, the faculty most neglected in modern western society is not so much spirit, as soul, where Jung spoke about the true self to denote the unfathomed and unpredictable part of our make-up which erupts inconveniently into our orderly ideas of a successful career or satisfactory relationships.

This faculty of soul, much of which is buried in unconsciousness, links us with human beings of former times and the myths they threw up to articulate their imaginative and religious explorations. He appeals for an appreciation of the idea of polytheism, not in the sense of a belief in the objective existence of many gods, but because they are traditional foci for the very various tendencies of our own inner life. Negative passions and emotions, like rage or depression, may yield meaning and usefulness when we think of them as the due of gods like Mars and Saturn. The nautical adventures of the wandering Odysseus are an image for all our wanderings in obscure inner pathways which build up our knowledge of the elusive but indispensable world of soul.

According to Moore, Odysseus is learning how to become a real father, in the sense of following his own father's steps and being a helpful guide to his son.

If the sea is a powerful image for the inner adventure of self-discovery, because of its vast extent and endless possibility, it is also a challenge to scientific investigation which seeks to understand and explain all terrestrial as well as celestial phenomena. In his book *The Bermuda Triangle* Charles Berlitz writes of ocean mysteries from a scientific point of view, focusing particularly on areas in the south of the north Atlantic from which strange reports have come, ever since Columbus sailed that way. There is some incidence of the inexplicable disappearance of good ships in perfect weather conditions everywhere in the world's oceans, but the area south-west of Bermuda and extending to the Bahamas and the southern tip of Florida has far more than a typical share. Berlitz catalogues lists of ships and also planes which have vanished without leaving the smallest trace of floating wreckage or of oil slick, and goes on to list accounts of seamen or pilots who have come out alive after experiencing unaccountable malfunctioning of all their instruments and other phenomena typical of the area.

He next proceeds to speculate upon possible explanations, mentioning an American clairvoyant, Edgar Cayce, who died in 1945, and the legends of the lost continent of Atlantis, supposed to have been suddenly engulfed by the sea in a huge catastrophe, about twelve thousand years BC. He links Plato's account of this event in the *Timaeus* with the end of the Third Ice Age, when the sea is thought to have risen as much as six hundred feet worldwide with the melting of the huge glaciated area in the northern hemisphere. Berlitz admits that Cayce's belief in reincarnation and his assertion that many of those who came to him for healing had formerly existed as citizens of the lost continent or large island is a barrier to critical scientific minds and orthodox religious believers alike. He explains that this need not invalidate Cayce's perceptions of the achievements of Atlantean civilisation, as literal reincarnation can be interpreted as our inheritance of our ancient ancestors' experience through our genes.

Cayce always gave his accounts of Atlantis under trance, being not much interested in the matter in his own waking consciousness. He described the technology of this advanced civilisation as being rather ahead of modern western achievements. He said they had a tremendous central power source which they used for many purposes, including air, surface and underwater travel, for what are now called radio and television and even for the control and manipulation of the lives and brains of their citizens. He said that they became proud and overconfident and abused their great powers, upsetting the balance of nature and unleashing destructive forces in the environment which finally engulfed them. In spite of this, some kind of suppressed continuation of their activities has gone on from underneath the sea, including the great concentration of some kind of electro-magnetic power which might account for the wild behaviour of compasses in this area and the temporary failure of all electrical appliances, sometimes noticed in planes and ships.

Berlitz, writing in 1974, noted that since 1958, extensive ruins of man-made artefacts have become un-silted in the Caribbean area, as well as other parts of the Atlantic such as the Azores islands in the east. Straight walls, pavements, and lines of columns cannot be natural rock formations of the sea bottom. The rest of the book is a wider survey of the many mysteries of prehistory throughout the world, and of certain inscrutable archaeological anomalies. The upshot is a theory that a civilisation older than any known to us may have existed which had a technology comparable to ours but which somehow met an end so devastating that only slight clues to their existence can be found. This makes absolute proof a very difficult matter, but as a hypothesis it cannot be dismissed out of hand.

The Indian epic, the Mahabharata, may be based on a verbal tradition much older than its present written form. It contains passages which seem to be describing heavier than air flight on the part of some of the personages in it. Others even appear to be recounting battles using atomic weapons, complete with mushroom clouds. Such passages were a puzzle to the earliest western translators in the last century, as our civilisation had not quite progressed to the point of making such achievements possible. Literature, however hallowed and ancient, does not constitute proof of what it describes, but Berlitz recalls the result of a dig in Mesopotamia which went through all the various levels of civilisations known to archaeologists in one very ancient site of settlement. After the very deepest layer was penetrated, there was found underneath the same kind of glass which remains in the Nevada desert after the testing of a nuclear warhead, and in no other known situation.

So far in this chapter we have seen the sea from the points of view of a poet, a psychologist and a scientific writer. A fourth approach is that of a novelist, Richard Adams, explored in his profound and gripping, if somewhat shattering, book *The Girl in the Swing*. The experiences which Adams attributes to his chief character, who clearly has much in common with himself, are closer to Calvino's folktale The Ship with Three Decks. For him the world of water is a feminine symbol, of great positive power and significance, but also containing darkness and menace. The story opens at the end of a circle which is also the beginning. The scene is an ordinary English garden in summer, but the impressions it gives, of trees and vegetation waving in the wind, are likened to an area of the sea bottom, clothed with underwater plants which ceaseless currents never allow to be still.

The character and development of Alan Desland then proceed to unfold at great length. He seems marked out for outstanding ordinariness of a typically English kind, even when he gets to the famous public school of Bradfield and is innocently involved in messing about in connection with the replica Greek amphitheatre in the grounds, and running errands for those engaged in the productions. There seems nothing, even in this, to shatter his childhood security, yet the time comes, through the irresponsibility of one of the masters and his wife, when Alan discovers an unusual psychic sensitivity in himself of a most unpleasant kind. The main theme of the novel is Alan's encounter with the Danish woman, Karin, who belongs somehow in the world of water. In her is concentrated all the attractiveness of women, in rather the same way in which a deity carries all the attributes and stature to which human worshippers can aspire. Yet she has a very dark side, also equally involved with the sea. As the Greek heroes he saw in the Bradfield stone theatre were bound by fate to their tragic destiny, so Alan is swept into his hasty marriage with Karin, knowing nothing of her origins or recent history, and not wanting to discover them.

Karin's mysterious past is never revealed. She has committed the crime of infanticide by drowning, but her no doubt tragic story is never produced in extenuation, to explain what could have driven such an epitome of love and affection to pitiless killing. She is really a goddess figure, and one does not excuse the actions of such beings with human considerations. Desland alludes darkly somewhere to the practice of child sacrifice in the worship of Venus. Karin never makes a head-on confrontation with the church, but she rejects his rather unthinking assumption that they should be married in church. In the end, the wedding takes place in Florida and is followed by an idyllic period of amorous adventure, in which freshwater swimming figures largely. Desland's tensions and ambiguities about their relationship render him at first impotent and ashamed, but Karin takes all this in her stride, causing him to relax and call on a deeper, more primeval level of being.

The third task which Aphrodite lays upon Psyche in the myth concerns water. From this episode derives the famous Grimm's folktale known as The Water of Life. This also contains elements reminiscent of Psyche's further, separate undertaking to cross the River of Death in Charon's boat, brave the ferocious dog Cerberus and descend into the Underworld. Lewis puts a river between Orual and Psyche, which symbolises the separation of their levels of consciousness. It is the water which cuts off spiritual understanding from an ordinary, egoistic view of things. Psyche's palace is quite invisible to Orual and she cannot believe in it, yet from across the river, after a bitter parting from her beloved younger sister, she catches sight for a moment of the whole edifice appearing out of a swirling mist, like the towers and turrets seen in cumulonimbus cloud, whose shapes are vanishing and short-lived.

CHAPTER THREE

Rivers of Life and Death

— ✄ —

After the burial of a sister in the Abbey graveyard, I had a brief but memorable dream. I was standing beside a lot of dark water, brown and opaque. On it was a small boat, rather round-shaped, like a coracle. I desired intensely to ride in this, but people standing around said that it would only sink under my weight, because it was for the use of those who had left their bodies. I ignored this, feeling sure I could use the boat. I stepped in and it went forward on the current. Then I found the bystanders had been right. The small craft sank slowly under me. I thought I would have a swim instead, but as I was fully clothed and shod, I did not even float, but began going down in the dark waters. At this embarrassing moment I fortunately woke up.

Aphrodite sends Psyche to fill a bottle with water from a mountain which is the source of the rivers of hell, Styx and Cocytus. This water is sacred and taboo. It is not only dangerous to approach because of the precipitous height, but is guarded by fierce Dragons as well. Only a bird, coming from above in the air, can manage to fill the bottle. From this episode derives the German tale of the sick king with three sons who set out in turn to search for something called 'The Water of Life'. Only the youngest prince is good enough to succeed in the difficult quest, the others having been too haughty to obtain the indispensable help of a dwarf. When Psyche sets out for the Underworld, she is warned to take loaves in each hand for the dog Cerberus, and halfpennies in her mouth to pay Charon, the ferryman. The dwarf tells the prince to have two loaves to appease two fierce lions which guard the water from the fountain in the courtyard of an enchanted castle. Before finding the water, he comes upon a maiden standing in a room. This woman derives from the figure of Psyche and is able to give him further instructions about the conditions under which he can carry off some of the precious liquid.

The Italian tale which most nearly corresponds to this German one is called The Sleeping Queen. When Psyche returns from Hades with a mysterious box in which Proserpine is supposed to have enclosed some of her beauty for the improvement of Aphrodite, she is overcome with curiosity and looks inside. At once, a deadly, death-like sleep overpowers her. Nothing can wake her from this except the supernatural intervention of Eros and Jupiter himself, King of Gods. From this unnatural and threatening sleep of Psyche derives our story of The Sleeping Beauty, familiar from childhood in the version told by Charles Perrault.

The spindle in this story which brings on sleep derives from Eros's arrow whose prick wakes Psyche from death and gives immortality. In The Sleeping Queen there is no spindle, but an evil enchantment of Morgan le Fay. The story starts with a blind king needing Water of Life to restore his sight and the two elder of three princes becoming diverted from the quest of it. The youngest, given the name of Andrew, has long journeys over sea and land and comes to the palace where everyone is in a state of suspended animation and no one can answer a word to his inquiries.

In the myth, Psyche has conceived during her ecstatic life with Eros in his palace and her subsequent toils are undertaken in a state of pregnancy. In The Sleeping Queen, Andrew passes the night in the queen's bed without rousing her and next day obtains the water which restores sight without waking anyone in the place. Only the subsequent birth of his child to the queen after nine months breaks the evil enchantment and sets in motion all the people of the court, who have been held like living statues in whatever state the spell found them. It is not likely that the anonymous originators of such popular tales had a full version of the original myth before them. They may not have been literate. The ancient material undergoes great changes which make the results seem garbled, confusing and less meaningful than the original. The fact that it survived at all, however, testifies to the trans-cultural power and significance of the types and symbols of the story. They articulate basic truths of the human psyche in connection with the quest for a higher level of consciousness and spiritual achievement.

CS Lewis and some of the friends in his literary circle in Oxford University in the 1930s and '40s were attempting something similar but much more conscious and sophisticated in the myths and stories they created with one another's encouragement. In *Out of the Silent Planet,* Lewis's experiment in the currently fashionable genre of space fiction, he consciously projects the inner condition of humanity into outer space. It is a mistake to think that contemporary space probes which, in the twenty-first century, are giving us more accurate information about actual conditions on the planets which are our closest neighbours in the solar system, invalidate Lewis's fantasies about life on Mars. He must have known it would become possible literally to disprove the results of his rich imagination. The planetary worlds are like the purely imaginary settings of his 'Narnia' books for children in providing an outer space to express inner reality.

In her monograph on Charles Williams's novels, *Through Defeat to Joy*, the American Jungian analyst Helen Luke sees most of these as concerned with the use and nature of kinds of power. There is egotistic power which seeks to dominate and control our environment and other people, and sacrificial, selfless power, like that of Christ on the Cross. The themes of Lewis's planetary novels are similar to this. The planet Venus, or *Perelandra*, is the scene of a re-enactment of the events at the beginning of the Bible, in the story of Creation and the Fall in the book of Genesis. Both Williams and Lewis, as experts in literature, would have been thoroughly familiar with John Milton's grand epic *Paradise Lost*, in which the fall of Adam in Eden is set against the background of the corruption of Lucifer and his followers, who become Satan and the dark host. In *Perelandra* the role of the devil in tempting Eve is played by a modern professor of physics whose attitude to astronomical exploration is crudely exploitative. Satan himself is the 'oyarsa' or being in charge of Thulcandra, which corresponds to the planet Earth.

As Milton wrote at a time when the traditional view of the Earth as the centre round which the sun, planets and stars revolved was being challenged by the investigations of astronomers with telescopes, it is interesting to see how discussions of these matters are interwoven with biblical material in *Paradise Lost*. He warns that we should not get too excited about such matters, but should keep the abiding truths of Christianity uppermost in our minds, yet keeps reverting to descriptions of sunrise and sunset in which the possibility that they are the effect of the daily revolution of the Earth on its axis is set against the idea of the sun actually moving round it, without deciding which he thinks is right. In any case, he undoubtedly presents the world as a sphere, instead of the flat area envisaged by the authors of the biblical Creation narratives in Genesis. Thus when Satan approaches the Earthly Paradise, he comes, not down from sky or up from underground, but from outer space in the manner of a modern astronaut returning to base. For such reasons, *Paradise Lost* might be regarded as an ancestor of the genre of science fiction.

In his book *The Hero with a Thousand Faces*, Joseph Campbell writes of the ongoing need for valid myth in our time:

> It would not be too much to say that myth is the secret opening through which the inexhaustible energies or the cosmos pour into human cultural manifestation. Religions, philosophies, arts, the social forms of primitive and historic man, prime discoveries in science and technology, the very dreams that blister sleep, boil up from the basic, magic ring of myth. (p.3)

Further:

In the absence of an effective general mythology, each of us has his private, unrecognised, rudimentary, yet secretly potent pantheon of dream. The latest incarnation of Oedipus, the continued romance of Beauty and the Beast, stand this afternoon on the corner of Forty-second Street, waiting for the traffic lights to change. (p.4)

In her already mentioned monograph on the novels of Charles Williams in the light of Jungian thought, Helen Luke writes:

Williams spoke from within the Christian church through the poetic imagination, Jung from outside it through psychological thought and practice, but both were aware of the need for a renewal, a rebirth, indeed, of the Christian myth in this time of transition to a new age. The lack of a developing myth, together with repression of the values of the feminine and of the flesh, was Jung's explanation of the frequent sterility of Christian teaching. All William's novels celebrate the holiness of the flesh, the beauty of matter and the essential values of feeling. Moreover, like Jung, he leaves us in no doubt of the reality of evil and the part it must play in the process of redemption, or individuation, and he points clearly and repeatedly to the 'coincidentia oppositorum' in the image of God. His work is a great contribution to the revitalising of the Christian myth. (Introduction, p.vi)

In his marvellous fantasy of *Perelandra*, the Planet of Love, with its beings on various levels, visible and hardly visible, CS Lewis is not escaping from the boredom of ordinary, terrestrial life. He is expressing profound insight into the powers of our human body and soul and the wonders which surround but often escape our limited, self-centred attention. In his novel *The Place of the Lion*, Charles Williams uses the Genesis myth in a different, yet related, way. Here, too, is the interaction between modes of being and kinds of energy, as Platonic ideas of dangerous potency are loosed on erring mortals in ordinary modern existence, finding out fatal weakness of character, or enhancing a hesitant willingness for self-transcendence till it becomes heroic strength by the infusion of the Holy Spirit. Here Paradise is not a different place, let alone another planet, but extraordinariness is allowed temporarily to overwhelm and threaten the usual arena of monotonous, but reassuring and protective, routine.

At the beginning of the twenty-first century, even more than when Williams and Lewis were working as what might be termed 'myth-wrights', a great gulf is fixed between science and the rest of knowledge. A cultured scientist might venture opinions in print about philosophy or literature, but a non-professional would be rash to pronounce on the latest development in physics or mathematics. Yet the results of theoretical scientific discovery have vast influence over the everyday lives of everyone in our society, from benevolent conveniences like the telephone or fax machines, to environment-threatening menaces like nuclear bombs and missiles. Generally speaking, developments in physics over the last century and more have revolutionised the whole concept of matter and the nature of the world. Einstein's General Theory of Relativity has changed the old views of space and time as separate entities and Quantum Mechanics has shown us that nothing is solid or predictable.

In her helpful and inspiring book *Science and the Soul*, Angela Tilby takes the reader through some of the most momentous discoveries of modern times and shows what the repercussions have been for religious belief and thought. In Chapter Six she mentions discoveries about electro-magnetism and light which revealed a mystery about whether these consisted of waves or particles. Later, this duality was found to extend to the structure of all atoms of matter. Summing up these results, she writes:

> The shocking fact remains: go deeper and deeper into the concrete world of tables and chairs; go beyond individual molecules to the bonded atoms that make them up; go inside the world of the atom – and the solidity disappears. Instead of ending up with a world of tiny discrete building blocks, you come to a seething turbulence of possibility. The classical world of solid objects and fixed laws has somehow sprung from this ghostly Underworld. The philosophical problem, is to understand how the two worlds relate to each other. (p.147)

CHAPTER FOUR

The Energy of the Centre
— ❧ —

The Greek word 'atom' means indivisible and, up till about a century ago, these particles were thought to be solid and to be the basic material from which everything in the physical world was built up. In 1897 Joseph John Thompson discovered the existence of a subatomic particle which he called an electron. Not long afterwards, James Clerk Maxwell made a study of the composition of light which revealed that it consists of waves which are electro-magnetic ripples of energy. He also studied other kinds of electro-magnetic wave, such as X-rays and gamma rays at higher frequencies, and radio waves at lower ones. Further studies by other scientists into the nature and behaviour of heat energy produced anomalous results. The physicist Max Planck sought a mathematical formula to resolve them. He postulated that 'at different frequencies energy changed not smoothly, but in pre-set jumps', small discreet units which he gave the name 'quanta'. Energy increased as the wave-length became shorter, so that 'a quantum of ultra-violet light was much more energetic than a quantum of red light'. Planck did not like his theory of 'jumps', but it worked, and in 1905 Einstein applied it to his own study of light waves. He found that light, too, appeared to come in 'bullet-like packets', 'quanta'. To these he gave the name 'photons'.

In 1911 Ernest Rutherford, a New Zealander, 'discovered that the positive charge in an atom was concentrated in a point at the... centre'. This was the atomic nucleus. With reference to Thompson's previous discovery of the electron, it now became possible to visualise the structure of an atom. It seemed to resemble a microcosmic solar system, with electrons orbiting the nucleus, like planets circling round the sun. If this were really so, however, the electrons would collapse inwards onto the nucleus as they lost energy. The Danish physicist, Niels Bohr, suggested that the quantum theory might apply here too. This brought the mysterious wave/particle duality already encountered in the study of light into the subatomic scene in general. Now experiments were set up in which a stream of photons or electrons was aimed at a metal plate with two slits in it. Beyond was a screen where the electrons flashed on arrival. If one slit was closed, the electrons reached the screen as individual particles. If both slits were open the pattern on the screen was that of waves.

This work of subatomic investigation studies a world far smaller than even the most powerful microscope would reveal and runs into trouble with the structure of light, since light is needed to show the investigator what is sought. The process taking place in the particle investigation itself disturbs what might be their normal behaviour anywhere else. Werner Heisenberg, reflecting on these problems, evolved his famous 'uncertainty principle'. Radiation used in the two slit experiment to show which slit the particles go through destroyed the pattern on the screen in the process. Heisenberg suggested that, without this illuminating factor, the electrons would *actually pass through both slits at once*. Electrons move round their nucleus, not in unalterable paths like the planets, but in apparently arbitrary and unpredictable jumps. This is where the study of quantum mechanics undermines the whole idea of matter built up from solid, indivisible atoms. Instead, it gives a picture of tremendous energies everywhere, always on the move. Niels Bohr came to the conclusion that the wave/particle paradox could not be resolved and 'articulated the principle of complementarity'. In 1928 Paul Dirac presented a quantum field theory in a mathematical formula which allowed for the duality 'without appeal to paradox or mystery'.

The sophistication and expense of the equipment necessary for the study of subatomic physics is mind-boggling and its continuance seems under threat in the apparently declining state of European economies as we enter the twenty-first century. Those who specialise in such studies and keep evolving further theories seem godlike and remote to the normal run of humanity, and their assertions cannot be tested by us, except perhaps through use of the technology which may arise from their discoveries. There are, however, simpler and cheaper kinds of investigation which may illustrate the behaviour of electro-magnetic fields outside the university laboratory. In his book *Ley Lines, their Nature and their Properties, a Dowser's Investigation,* J Havelock Fidler describes the technique of picking up energy fields with the use of a pendulum which could not be simpler for anyone to make. This area of research is derided by conventional physicists, on the grounds that its results are highly variable. In view of the situation in the world of subatomic particles where all is whirling, unpredictable energy, such a dismissive attitude seems unjustified.

Energy dowsers have discovered that everything in our environment, as well as human beings themselves, is surrounded by an energy field of some kind, which causes a pendulum held in the fingers of some individuals to oscillate from side to side or gyrate in a circle. Fidler quotes TC Lechbridge as having established a whole series of different lengths of pendulum for different substances, which indicates the size of the 'electromagnetic' field for each. Faintly tingling sensations in the dowser's hand and arm suggest a mild electric current, but this kind of energy is not electromagnetic in the sense in which an ordinary electrician or physicist uses the term. The most widely known type of dowser is a 'water-diviner' who can use some kind of spring mechanism to detect water underground. It is also generally known that some individuals can also pick up minerals, or archaeological remains, in the field or even just by studying a map indoors in a different area from the substance, or object, sought. Perhaps less known is the fact that, besides water lines underground, there are other lines which affect the spring rods of dowsers in a similar way. One of these is the so-called ley line across the countryside which has been found to link megalithic monuments and other old stone buildings or ruins.

Fidler describes many highly disciplined scientific experiments in the area of north-west Scotland where he lives, on lines connecting the great number of standing stones set up there by megalithic man. A Cambridge-trained scientist with a career in agricultural advice service behind him, he is far from conforming to the popular image of a psychic crank. The book does not romanticise woolly intuitions, but is tough reading for those with unmathematical minds. The megaliths do not have charges of their own accord, but have received a human charge from the people who set them up which has become fixed in perpetuity through the millennia. As they lived before written history, their motives are hard to establish. Dowsers who risk more subjective pronouncements than Fidler have found the charges distinctly evil, at least in some places. Some people claim to be affected by illness or depression because an alleged ley line runs through their house. Such lines are also thought to have an adverse effect on the growth of plants and trees. Fidler set up experiments with seed germination which seemed to bear this out.

Not so impressive as the rest of the book is the description at the end of an experiment with the author and his helpers in which their charge is assumed to be just as malign as that left in stones by humans of the remote past. This shows the characteristic weakness of the 'objectivity' claimed by scientists, which ignores moral values or subjective impressions. In view of the way plants and trees flourish in the care of many contemporary humans, it can hardly be assumed that they emanate a charge inimical to plant germination and fertility, and what of the healing gift of people which is mediated through their hands, laid on those who are afflicted in mind or body? It also seems too pessimistic to lump together Christian hallowed sites with pre-Christian megalithic monuments, as transmitting charges which have deleterious effects. Those sensitives who claim to be able to see the magnetic field or aura surrounding a human being, say that these are not all the same, but can be dark or bright, not arbitrarily, but according to the inner disposition and motives of the individual.

From the work of both subatomic physicists and energy

dowsers, it seems that the behaviour of all particles of matter is similar to those of light, which can be observed by anyone. Candle flames and some kinds of electric light, if watched steadily for a while, can be seen to send out rays in all directions from a centre. Such effects of radiation from a natural source, like the sun or flames, or from a person of outstanding spiritual power, can be seen in the works of great artists. Rembrandt's painting The Deposition of Christ from the Cross, of which the original hangs in New York, is all dark except for the dead body which is the only source of light in the picture. From it, illumination falls on the faces, hands and feet of men who lower it from above, or support it from below, and on the face and shoulders of Mary, Christ's mother, who is fainting into the arms of other women. Very similar is the effect of *Noli me tangere*, Rembrandt's rendering of the appearance of the risen Christ to Mary Magdalene. Again, all is darkness, except for Christ in white garments which he is gently holding away from Mary's outstretched arms. Light from him illuminates her face and torso only, as she looks towards him in mingled joy and fear. This painting is reproduced in black and white in *The Picture of Christ* by Wilhelm Kelber, which also has two different renderings by Rembrandt of the supper at Emmaus. In one, Christ is at the centre, with rays of light streaming out towards the disciples. In the other, his chair is on the right, but there is no figure in it, only a burst of supernatural radiance, with the arm of the chair dark against it.

Frances Banks, the ex-nun with a missionary attitude to psychic perception, wrote of what she called the 'knack' of seeing auras around things and people. She said this gave them a sort of fuzzy edge, like things depicted in a Van Gogh painting. Timothy Hyman, writing in *Prophecy and Vision*, a record in words and pictures of an exhibition on religion and art in Bristol in 1982, describes Van Gogh as the 'founding spirit' of the Expressionist school of modern painting. He was a religious man who wished to find an expression for spiritual insight in his painting. He did it, not by sticking to traditional religious motifs, but by using the very texture of paint to affirm a sacred significance in ordinary scenes. Hyman quotes Van Gogh's verbal expression of this intention:

> I want to paint men and women with that something of the
> eternal which the halo used to symbolise, but which we now seek
> to confer through the actual radiance of our colour vibrations.

The traditional role of art in connection with religion is to affirm
and celebrate cosmic order and harmony. The problem which
besets the relations between the two in the modern situation is
that a religious view has to proclaim a good deal of chaos and
disharmony. Artists and religious believers alike find much to
criticise and lament in the human situation with regard to the
environment. In another article in the Bristol book mentioned
above, called 'Vision and Prophecy in the Arts', John Allitt writes
of the art of prehistoric peoples found in caves in different parts of
the world:

> Cave art is visionary; study has shown how men's earliest artistic
> expression reveals a cosmic view of the universe, an attempt to
> understand the meaning and purpose of life and death, the nature
> of the sacrifice of the animal providing man with his food.

Such 'primitive' art, and also that of early civilisations like that of
Egypt, give expression to the insights of the whole community,
not just the individual who is the artist.

> Thus to fall out of right relationship with nature indicates that
> man has already fallen foul within himself, vision (union) has
> become division. The important insight of the early civilisations
> was the realisation that nature for all its plurality, fertility,
> manifoldness was a cosmic unity.

Allitt also mentions traditional pattern-making based on natural
forms and finding spiritually significant shapes in them, most
notably the mandala, which proclaims the right relationship of
everything to a sacred centre.

> Nature is the centre, the mandala for our own orientation and a
> theology which does not recognise this is false and can breed a
> negative dualism. Modern man must consider anew the miracle
> of the creation, for it is a reflection of the mind of the Creator.
> Our forefathers looked well at the forms of flowers, shells, seeds,

the patterns left by the wind or sea on the sand, the courses of the stars in the heavens, the gyrations of the planets.

In the deepest centre of our being can be found the stillness around which whirls the dance of our own and every other being. We can attain to occasional awareness of the tremendous life-renewing quality of this centre by a determined practice of inner listening, without having to become perfect saints or martyrs first. It is simply the way we are and the way everything is at its deepest level and we arrive as much by relaxation as by struggle. Yet the cost of such awareness is surrender of every resentment against others or at what seems to be our fate and also of all our obstinate preconceptions. New insight can flood our minds like refreshing wine only when we let go of the intellectual constructs by which we seek to explain our experiences, at least temporarily, in order to practice receptive silence. Such self-loss corresponds to the ordeals of the heroes of myth, or to their death and re-vivification. The beliefs and practices of the once-despised indigenous peoples of the Earth can help us here. Through them our own lost ancestors of the Palaeolithic era can exhort and admonish us in our contemporary situation.

CHAPTER FIVE

Travels in Space and Time
— ✥ —

In her unique and unforgettable book *Mutant Message Down-under*, the American Marlo Morgan writes of being suddenly presented with an opportunity to shed the trappings of the twentieth century and step abruptly into the world of the Stone Age. After initiating a project for promoting self-help and self-respect among the marginalised Aboriginal population of an unnamed Australian city, she had a phone call asking her to receive some sort of accolade from a tribe in the Australian outback which was in touch with the city dwellers among whom she had worked. She accepted, flew out and installed herself in a hotel room. She was picked up by an uncommunicative black man in a jeep. Her neat and elegant clothes had suffered a good deal in the intense heat by the time the vehicle had left the beaten track and stopped in the wilds of real desert, but there was worse to come. She was received by members of a group of native people, not one of whom spoke English except the driver who became her interpreter. Somehow it was made clear to her that she would not be accepted unless she took off everything and replaced it with minimal attire provided by her hosts. Every article of clothing went into a ceremonial fire kindled for the purpose. Shoes, stockings, even her jewelled watch and wedding ring joined the blaze.

After significant ceremonies in a small hut, the group announced that they were taking off at once into the outback without provisions or equipment of any sort. Completely unprepared for such a searching ordeal, Marlo said she could not join them and remained behind. As she did not know where she was, and could not return to civilisation without their help, however, such a protest was unrealistic. She had put her hand to the plough when she first agreed to join them and had to trust them now. She went after them, finding the ground hot and rough to her bare feet. When she asked how long the walkabout would last, they said three full changes of the moon. They tried to convey to her that she was receiving a rare and priceless spiritual privilege, but her mind was on practicalities and physical hardship and she set out telling herself that she would have to make them return her to her hotel the next day, if not the same night. At the level of the body and conscious mind, this experience was alien and threatening, yet Marlo had already, early in her time in Australia, received a strange intimation of spiritual kinship with the Aboriginals and their beliefs.

She had made an appointment with a friend at a tearoom where fortunes were told. Marlo was prompt but her friend never arrived. She was about to stop waiting and leave, when a young man entered and sat down in front of her. He was 'dark-complexioned', but dressed entirely in white. He took her hand, as though to read the palm, but looked straight into her face and told her that her presence in Australia was the result of destiny.

> There is someone here you have agreed to meet for your mutual benefit. The agreement was made before either of you were born. In fact, you chose to be born at the same instant, one on top of the world and the other here, down under. The pact was made on the highest level of your eternal self. You agreed not to seek one another till fifty years had passed. It is now time. When you meet, there will be instant recognition on a soul level. This is all I can tell you.

All this was unintelligible to Marlo at the time, but the atmosphere of the speaker was reassuring to her and she could not dismiss what was said as quackery. When she told her friend of her experience, that lady contacted the tearoom, but found out that they only had female fortune-tellers and the afternoon of their appointment it was the turn of one who did not read palms but used cards. The man Marlo had met there was not known to the establishment.

The book unfolds a wealth of spiritual wisdom. The group has the deepest reverence for their fragile environment. Edible roots which are mature for eating are identified by dowsing with hands sensitive to the kind of radiation they give off. Unripe ones are left for those who may follow. Underground water is discovered in the same way and sucked sparingly through a tube. The source is never used up for the same reason. The varied gifts of group members are brought out and appreciated. Evenings are enlivened with story telling and music. The impression grows that these people are very virtuous and self-sacrificing, even for primitives uncorrupted by modern civilisation. It emerges that they have embraced celibacy because of their necessarily deteriorating surroundings. There are no young children, only a boy of thirteen and adults of various ages. They will die out as the outback becomes unable to sustain them. Meanwhile they are aware of a clear spiritual mission which is an antidote to the environment-ruining and unsustainable character of the white man's lifestyle.

As Marlo's initiation proceeds and she becomes physically tougher and spiritually wiser, she is made aware that the individual mentioned in the tea room prophesy is the elder and leader of the group. After a crisis point when water fails altogether and Marlo feels that death by slow desiccation is to be her end, they come to a body of water large enough to contain crocodiles and all the aquatic life necessary to sustain them. After driving out the reptiles by spiritual authority, the humans can safely enjoy a wonderful soak which has the quality of a real resurrection experience. Later Marlo is shown an underground cave centre for preserving the traditions of those who call themselves the Real People. All her ordeals and privations seem more than worthwhile when Mario is enriched beyond imagination by sharing this heritage. After this, the very embarrassing experience of going alone into a small town in a near naked condition and having to beg the price of a phone call, to summon help from her friends, from a startled and suspicious householder, can be taken in her stride. It is she who is rich and fulfilled after receiving revelations which will shape her whole future life according to an infinitely satisfying eternal purpose.

The first two stories in this book are based on Italian folktales which, like the Narnia series of books by CS Lewis, take us from our ordinary, external world into a different, inner dimension. Those tales, in their turn, retold for their contemporaries parts of the Psyche and Eros myth of the soul's journey towards God. My third one has different models, but does not really depart from the original theme. After living with Eros in his palace and then journeying the world and performing heroic labours, Psyche is sent by the wrathful Aphrodite to Hades to bring back some of the beauty of its queen, Persephone, in a box. She succeeds with great bravery in performing this feat, but cannot resist opening the box on her way back. It contains death, as a sleep from which no mortal can wake her. She falls unconscious and only wakes when Eros comes and pricks her with one of his arrows of love. Her life on Earth is over, and she is made the immortal bride of the god. This ending to the myth corresponds to the great theme of the letting go of life on a lower level in order to take it up in the fullness of immortality which is the centre of the Christian religion and is echoed, in different modes, in all great world religions and even modern ideologies.

In his novel *Perelandra*, the centre of a trilogy, CS Lewis takes the great Biblical theme of the Creation by God of an excellent world which is somehow invaded by a mysterious contrary power, and sets it on another planet. His account of Paradise does not end with the devil succeeding in making Eve fall and take Adam with her, to be expelled into a bitter world of death and suffering where individuals are replaced by following generations. In his novel the role of the devil is performed by a power-seeking and manipulative Earthman, but Ransom, the significantly named Christ figure in the story, arrives by divine arrangement on the Paradise planet *Perelandra* in time to witness and thwart his machinations. This is only possible because the original fall and redemption drama has been acted out on Thulcandra, the name for Earth in this trilogy. In spite of the Earth people having been 'saved' by the redeeming work of Christ, Thulcandra is described as opaque to the vision of the other planets, still surrounded by clouds of darkness and harbouring the evil power whose ambition is to extend his influence throughout the solar system, and ultimately beyond.

My story, 'The Rainbow Planet', is heavily indebted to these ideas, but the role of the eavesdropper in Eden passes to the girl Rhoda, the youngest of the three sisters who have appeared in 'The Invisible Palace' and 'The Unknown Island'.

The genre of science fiction burst upon the world in 1898 with the publication of *The War of the Worlds* by HG Wells. In this novel, the ordinariness of daily life in suburban Surrey is contrasted with an invasion of malevolent beings from Mars, getting ready for an assault on London, which they apparently know is the nerve centre of the whole life of the country. It all seems very old-fashioned and not worth getting worried about, as we know no such beings are to be feared from Mars or any other planet in the solar system, or anywhere near enough to be a base for an invasion. It has to be read as a description of something interior to humanity in order for its continuing relevance to be perceived. The Martians, it only appears some time after the invasion, when they emerge from pits made by the impact of their rockets, are all head and limbs, without torsos. This corresponds to our overemphasis on the intellect and its achievements in technology. Our link with the natural world in which our animal nature has its setting is in danger of becoming attenuated. Wells's Martians are caricatures of humanity in the twentieth century and after.

In 'The Rainbow Planet', Rhoda and her family find a world in which the splendour of inner space is revealed in the Paradise of the green circle, but also find evil and threatening dimensions in a red, desert area. When Rhoda plunges back alone in dream into the green world, it seems to be haunted from within in a more subtle and dangerous way than the invasion techniques of the red robots who have been defeated by powerful mobile trees. After wandering in a cooler, upland area, she comes upon standing stones in a circle. From these emerges a dangerous but not unattractive figure of a powerful magician. Through the agency of this being Rhoda finds herself in the warm Paradise again in which the lady of pearly skin is charming, with a flute, a snake who clearly embodies the same entity as the towering stone. This being claims to be able to take Rhoda not only through space with the speed of thought, but backwards in time to a vanished era. Science fiction novels have been preoccupied with the future problems of, or threats to, humanity, assuming the remote past to be a process of slow evolution from the Palaeolithic hunter-gatherer stage. In his novel *Link*, the American author Walt Becker focuses on the study of humanity's past, pleading for openness to a different attitude from the one which has become conventional.

The main characters are palaeontologists who come upon the remains of superior beings from beyond planet Earth who arrived to raise humans of an earlier type than Homo sapiens by teaching them many skills of civilisation and by intermarrying with them. Becker quotes much ancient literature from diverse sources which testify to superior beings with large eyes and dazzling faces who taught ordinary humans many arts and crafts, agriculture and technology. He also refers to the problem of how early humans moved huge stones into circles or buildings when they are supposed to have had nothing but armies of slaves, rollers and ropes. His extra-terrestrial beings, found first in Mali in North Africa and then in Bolivia on the South American continent, have a mysterious artefact, with something like nuclear power, which has huge potential for both benevolent and harmful use. He thus brings together the past and present of humanity and envisages the possibility that twentieth-century Homo sapiens is not the first or only being to discover and harness nuclear power. In this his thinking resembles that of Charles Berlitz, whose book I mentioned and discussed in Chapter Two. Berlitz thought in terms of an earlier Earthly civilisation which abused its technological prowess and can thus provide a warning to ourselves about the danger of ignoring nature's limits and balances. Becker thinks that evolutionary theory is inadequate to explain the sudden rise of civilisation in the Middle East and therefore envisages the incursion of superior beings from space.

It may be that the many serious science fiction writers of our time are the myth builders whose job it is to express in symbolic form the fears and spiritual aspirations of a scientific age. Becker's impassioned appeal for some sort of elder brother species in our human ancestry who can still be spiritual companions and guides worthy of respect in a sceptical culture is reminiscent of the third great figure in the circle to which CS Lewis and Charles Williams belonged, JRR Tolkien. The popular and gripping stories Tolkien published in his lifetime about hobbits and other mythical beings were undergirded by material which was left to his son, Christopher, to edit and make public after his death. *The Silmarillion* is one man's modern version of the sort of creation myths which have come down to us from the past of great civilisations. It's tone is very different to the child-like and uninhibited stories of the gods in ancient Greece or Egypt. There are none of the jokes and homely details which enliven *Farmer Giles of Ham* or *The Hobbit*, but a smooth, lofty poetic style which grows on the reader with an astounding imaginative power, until it is difficult to remember that all this is the invention of a single mind.

CHAPTER SIX

Creation

— ✖ —

T olkien, as a specialist in early language and literature at Oxford University, was in a position to create fictional old languages for his characters. The various sections of *The Silmarillion* are entitled with such words of his own devising. The first is 'Ainulindalë', as it concerns the 'Ainur' who correspond to both the many gods of early myth and the powers and angels mentioned in biblical sources. God is called Eru, which means the One, and is there before any other being.

He first produces other non-material beings with whom he shares thought in word and music. The whole material universe for Tolkien begins as melody, a beautiful and perhaps quite original idea, though he may have found some earlier parallel in his wide reading, some of it no doubt of very esoteric nature. Before ever the music heard by the Ainur has become a world which they can see, the most powerful of them, whose name is the first to be mentioned, has introduced a discord. Thus, according to Tolkien, the material creation was not originally perfect, but the whole drama of struggle between good and evil was potentially there in what he calls the Void inhabited by Eru, who is also called Iluvator.

Then the voices of the Ainur, like unto harps and lutes, and pipes and trumpets, and viols and organs, and like unto countless choirs singing with words, began to fashion the theme of Iluvator to a great music; and a sound arose of endless interchanging melodies woven in harmony that passed beyond hearing into the depths and into the heights, and the places of the dwelling of Iluvator were filled to overflowing, and the music and the echo of the music went out into the Void, and it was not void.

— ✧ —

But now Iluvator sat and hearkened, and for a great while it seemed good to him, for in the music there were no flaws. But as the theme progressed, it came into the heart of Melkor to interweave matters of his own imagining that were not in accord with the theme of Iluvator; for he sought therein to increase the power and glory of the part assigned to himself.

— ✧ —

...discord arose about him and many that sang nigh him grew despondent and their thought was disturbed and their music faltered; but some began to attune their music to his rather than to the thought which they had at first. Then the discord of Melkor spread ever wider, and the melodies which had been heard before foundered in a sea of turbulent sound.[1]

Iluvator counteracts the attempts of Melkor to disturb his harmonies, first in music of a new profundity and sadness, to reassure the ears of the Ainur, then in visions for their eyes of the future of a material creation in which the schemes of Melkor are made to serve his purpose.

Iluvator said again: 'Behold your Music! This is your minstrelsy; and each of you shall find contained herein, amid the design that I set before you, all those things which it may seem that he himself devised or added. And thou, Melkor, wilt discover all the secret thoughts of the whole thy mind, and wilt perceive that they are but a part of the whole and tributary to its glory.'[2]

In later parts of *The Silmarillion* which concern the material

---

[1] *The Silmarillion*, JRR Tolkien, Unwin Paperbacks, 1977, pp.15–16
[2] *Ibid*. p.18

creation and the heroic deeds of Elves and humans, the evil being who was called Melkor has become Morgoth, universally hated and dreaded. He is relegated to the north, a desolate mountainous area, and lurks in an underground stronghold. Unlike the Satans and black magicians of other literature, Tolkien's Devil is unglamorous and uninteresting. In the story of Beren and his love for Lúthien, Tolkien describes an assault on Morgoth to obtain one of the jewels called Silmarils which he has stolen from Elves and put in an iron crown on his head. Like the ring in the famous trilogy, these jewels symbolise all lust for possession and destructive power. They are like fire, or radioactivity and tend to destroy the flesh which grasps them.

> Then Beren and Lúthien went through the Gate and down the labyrinthine stairs; and together wrought the greatest deed that has been dared by Elves or Men. For they came to the seat of Morgoth in his nethermost hall that was upheld by horror, lit by fire, and filled with weapons of death and torment.[3]

Beren is disguised as a wolf but Lúthien's disguise is pierced by Morgoth's gaze. She is full of dazzling goodness, but he reacts with lust and desire for possession. As he does not attack, she casts a spell of blindness and sleep upon him and all his court. Then the infernal fires go out and only the radiance of the Silmarils is seen to dazzle the beholder.

> ...the burden of that crown and of the jewels bowed down his head, as though the world were set upon it, laden with a weight of care, of fear and of desire, that even the will of Morgoth could not support.

Lúthien springs into the air and throws him into a dream.

> Suddenly he fell, as a hill sliding in avalanche, and hurled like thunder from his throne lay prone upon the floor of hell. The iron crown rolled echoing from his head. All things were still.[4]

---

[3] *Ibid*. p.216
[4] *Ibid*. p.217

Beren is roused to cut out a jewel with a magic knife, named Angrist. The Silmaril makes his flesh translucent, but does not harm it. The peril is desire to take the other two jewels, instead of the one which Lúthien's father demanded before he could have her as wife. The knife slips, a shard of its blade rouses Morgoth and Beren and his Elf love flee in disorder, undisguised. The monstrous giant wolf, Carcharoth, who guards the gate springs upon them. Beren tries to use the Silmaril as a good power to quell its evil, but when he holds it up and says, 'Get you gone and fly... for here is a fire that shall consume you and all evil things', Carcharoth opens his jaws to bite off the hand holding the jewel and swallows all. He is burned up inside and runs away in madness, terrorising the countryside.

Lúthien cures the poisoned stump of Beren's hand and the lovers are saved from the hosts of Morgoth by three eagles, Thorndor and his vassals. Morgoth's fury causes a huge volcanic eruption, but the eagles soar above it and bring Lúthien to her father's land of Doriath and lay her down with Beren who is near death, but recovers. So the power of love overcomes evil, but the jewel is perilous to own or use. As Beren and Lúthien return to her father, the maddened wolf in his wanderings bursts on his territory. Asked by Thingol to produce the Silmaril as the price of Lúthien's hand, Beren holds up his right arm, displaying the stump. The grim old king is mellowed by this and listens to their story. Finally he agrees to their union. Beren must hunt the wolf, helped by Huan, his faithful wolfhound who understands human speech and three times in his life is permitted to speak it. Carcharoth is slain and opened and the incorrupt hand of Beren emerges, still grasping the Silmaril. The hand disintegrates at a touch, but Beren gives the jewel of his quest to Thingol, his father-in-law. He is a mortal and fatally wounded, and his dog, Huan, has preceded him, after his third and last utterance. Lúthien is immortal, being Elf, but chooses to follow her lover.

After the sections called Ainulindalë and Valaquenta, which deal with creation and the deeds of the various gods and lesser powers, *The Silmarillion* proceeds with a very long section called 'Quenta Silmarillion' from which the above story is taken. This deals with the children of Iluvator who are Elves and Men, with crossings of the Western Ocean and the migrations into Middle Earth on its eastern shore. This is followed by a fourth section called Akallafeth which concerns what is elsewhere referred to as the legend of the lost Atlantis. This is an island to which Tolkien gives many names, including Númenóre. Its inhabitants were Númenóreans, men guided to the land by the Valor, or heavenly powers, where they founded a great civilisation. For many centuries they were great and good, but in the end corrupt kings desired immortality instead of long life and one of them admitted Sauron, who was the servant of Morgoth, now defeated and banished. He caused the king to introduce the worship of Morgoth with human sacrifices into the holy temple of Númenóre. In the end the wrath of Eru was aroused against these impious people and a huge disaster stirred up the sea to cover the whole land for ever.

A devout remnant, who had taken to ships before the disaster, were driven before the wind eastwards to Middle Earth where they brought precious things to restart the tradition of their civilisation and continue the struggle against evil. A final section 'On the Rings of Power and the Third Age' completes the book and brings the story up to where *The Hobbit* continues it in a quite different and more humorous style.

In *The Left Hand of Darkness* the American writer, Ursula LeGuin, writes of two kinds of corrupt tyranny set on another planet called Gethen, or Winter, because it is colder than Earth. The first is a monarchy in the nation called Karhide with an unintelligent king who loves power and rules by caprice. The second is the totalitarian state of Orgoreyn with a secret police and the use of drugs to enforce conformity on its citizens. The emissary Genly Ai, representing the Ekumen of Known Worlds, finds that the latter is far worse and more dangerous than the first. In Karhide the prime minister, Estraven, seems enigmatic to Genly and he does not entirely trust him. They meet again when Estraven is disgraced and obliged to flee to Orgoreyn where Genly goes for experience of the planet, without realising how dangerous it is.

It is not till Genly has become a prisoner in the Orgoyen equivalent of a concentration camp and is rescued by Estraven at great risk to himself that he begins to realise the true stature of his friend. Together they escape across a waste of ice in the north which is also volcanic. This description recalls the ambiance of Tolkien's Morgoth in *The Silmarillion*. It is an environment hostile to human physical weakness but with the potential of strengthening the inner life of the heart and spirit. Through mistrust and misunderstanding, the two men from different parts of space come to a fruitful and joyful relationship in the face of shared adversity. When they reach Karhide, Estraven is soon murdered by border guards on the king's orders, but his sacrifice has brought back the envoy to the kingdom where he is at last received with fitting honour and condoled for his bad treatment in Orgoreyn. Previously both nations had opposed joining the Ekumen of Known Worlds, but now the king of Karhide wants to be the one to receive the spaceship Genly has already summoned by radio from Orgoreyn. The faction in that country opposed to the Ekumen also falls and is replaced by one in favour. Eleven envoys from different planets, Genly's colleagues, emerge from the ship and are received all over Gethen where it is to be hoped they will be an influence for a more enlightened level of civilisation.

After *The Left Hand of Darkness* and other science fiction novels, Ursula LeGuin went on to produce a trilogy of stories of Earthsea, to which a fourth book was finally added, about the same world and characters. Earthsea has some affinity with Tolkien's Middle Earth in its population of Wizards and Dragons. Instead of being set on a continent, it is an Archipelago of many islands in a great sea. In all these works she has continued the job of myth building for our times.

Another work of imagination featuring the mystery of a disappearing island has been produced by the Norwegian philosopher Jostein Gaarder. Like *The Hobbit* this is a real children's story. It is narrated in the first person by Hans Thomas, a small boy whose mother has deserted his father and himself to become a model in Greece. Together they set off across Europe by car from Norway in the hope of finding and bringing her back. Along the way Hans Thomas becomes aware of a series of clues, like those in a treasure hunt, leading him to unravel a mystery about a sailor's travels in an earlier century. It begins at a lonely filling station on the border with Switzerland. The attendant is a dwarf about Hans Thomas' height and seems very interested in the boy. He gives him a magnifying glass which he tells him he will be sure to need, and directs them to a village called Dorf where he advises they should stay.

The dwarf's involved directions make a whole day's drive out of the journey to Dorf, and Dad is so tired they are obliged to stay a whole day. While Dad indulges a boring taste for alcohol, Hans Thomas explores the tiny village and ends up at a baker's window where a goldfish swims in a bowl. The bowl has a piece missing from the rim exactly the size of the dwarf's magnifying glass, which suggests a connection. The rays of the setting sun catch it suddenly and bring out rainbow colours from the glass and water and the gleaming scales of the fish, swimming round and round. Hans Thomas sees an old man watching him from inside, who invites him in, gives him a drink and talks Norwegian enough to make him understand. When Dad comes to collect his son, the old man gives him four buns in a bag. Three are consumed before Dad falls asleep in the room they share at the inn, but the fourth Hans Thomas bites into in secret when he is hungry and wakeful. Something hard meets his teeth and he discovers a tiny book baked into the bun. The print is too small for his eyes, but he remembers the glass and finds it just readable with this. He begins to read an amazing narrative which the old baker has warned is for his eyes alone, not to be confided in Dad or any adult.

Hans Thomas learns from successive readings which punctuate the drive through the Italian Alps that whoever becomes baker in Dorf is also entrusted with the treasures brought back by a sailor in foreign seas. There are more bowls and many more fish in different rainbow colours and a mysterious drink which immediately alters the consciousness of anyone who takes the tiniest drop, as well as more usual items. Most precious of all is a pack of old, worn playing cards which feature amazingly in the sticky bun book. The narrative has been written by Ludwig, the baker Hans Thomas has met, and tells about how he inherited the shop and cabin further up the mountain, where the traveller's treasures are stored in the attic, from Albert Klages, who in his turn was befriended as a boy by a man known as Baker Hans. This was the sailor who in the autumn of 1847 set out from Rotterdam in a ship called the *Maria* which had a cargo for New York. Somehow, in spite of competent navigators, this ship went too far south, into the region of the Atlantic south of Bermuda. Then it was destroyed by a hurricane with the loss of all hands except Baker Hans who escaped in a lifeboat. Starving and exhausted, he sighted an island and struggled against an off-shore current to land on it. Eventually he succeeded and amazing adventures began.

The apparently tiny island expands as the sailor advances. As well as palm trees, the flowers of more temperate latitudes seem able to grow there and the bird song is varied and heavenly. A wonderful lake provides drink and bathing and a long rock tunnel ends in a fertile valley even more paradisal than what he has already seen. There are strange animals no zoologist on Earth has ever reported seeing. Finally he meets people and discovers they are playing cards come alive. After many wanderings a card introduces him to an old sailor they call Master. This Frode sailed from Veracruz in Mexico in a Spanish brig in 1790, headed for Cadiz in Spain with a cargo of silver. Somewhere between Puerto Rico and Bermuda the ship was wrecked and Frode, like Hans, found the island and survived on its varied fruits and vegetables. His only possession was a pack or Patience cards which wore out and nearly disintegrated during his fifty-two years on the island. One day, however, he saw figures he recognised as his cards and found he had fifty-two companions. One day Frode realises the sailor he has met must be his own grandson and they have a loving reunion.

In the end the cards, like those in *Alice in Wonderland*, turn hostile to the human in their midst and want to destroy Frode at a meeting called by the Joker, but his hour has arrived, fifty-two years after his arrival in the fateful year 1790, and he is found to have expired naturally while no one noticed. Things are very dangerous now for Hans and the Joker, and they escape with a goldfish in a bottle and other treasures of his. As they rush back to where Hans left his boat, the island is racked by noisy Earthquakes. It also shrinks in size, as it had initially expanded.

Hans meets the Ace of Hearts, a frail lady for whom he has a fondness. Then the whole pack come upon him, but turn back into cards which fly round him in a shower and drop on the ground. He gathers them all up and puts them in his pocket. By the time he joins the Joker in the boat, the island has finally vanished under the sea. Soon they are picked up by a Norwegian schooner en route to Marseille. There the Joker quickly vanishes and Hans makes his way to Dorf with his treasures, and opens the bakery.

CHAPTER SEVEN

Redemptive Sacrifice

— ✺ —

The narrative of the island in *The Solitaire Mystery* is interwoven with the account of the present-day journey of Hans Thomas and Dad. It is enjoyable at times. They tell themselves they are not counting on bringing back Anita, just going in her direction for a holiday. Nevertheless, as they finish the distance between Venice and Athens by taking a car ferry across the Adriatic Sea, tension mounts. Hans Thomas repeatedly catches sight of the small man who gave them petrol at the filling station on the northern Swiss border and directed them to Dorf. This does not encourage, but terrifies him, and he becomes quite overwrought and tearful. There are correspondances between the sticky bun story and incidents in the modern holiday. Dad and his son go to the ancient glass works on the Venetian island Murano and Hans Thomas reads of a glass works on the island south of Bermuda worked by some of Frode's playing card population. The Ace of Hearts in that pack has a tendency to get lost, which links her with the mother who has become a fashion model in a misguided attempt to find herself.

The voyage to the mysterious island in the ocean represents drawing on the deep resources of the unconscious mind as an important emotional crisis for the family approaches. In the end, they arrive just as Anita is ready to see her need for her own husband and son, even though there is some unpleasantness with her employers because she has signed a contract for a period not yet expired. After Hans Thomas and Ludwig the old baker have parted, they have worked out that they are related. Dad is the illegitimate son of a Norwegian woman persecuted for becoming pregnant by a German soldier during the Second World War. Ludwig is that soldier, who never knew of the pregnancy and birth of his son to Line. In the car on the return journey, Hans Thomas tries to convince his parents that the man in Dorf is his grandfather, but they are sceptical. When they arrive, there is no one at the bakery, but Dad is amazed to see his mother, Line, in the village. He rushes into her arms and she tells him the baker was indeed his father and her lover, but that he has just died.

One of Dad's foibles is to collect the jokers from packs of cards, as others collect stamps. This is ascribed to a certain affinity he feels with these maverick characters. The dwarf, who is visible only to the boy, is identified with the Joker character in the sticky bun story. Gaarder's cartomancy is based on the ordinary pack of fifty-two cards, but the importance of the joker figure recalls the most important card of the tarot arcana, known as The Fool.

One of Charles Williams' novels, *The Greater Trumps*, explores the significance of tarot symbolism for ordinary people in a modern life situation. The widower Lothair Coningsby lives with his sister Sybil and his son and daughter, Nancy, who is engaged to one Henry Lee, of gypsy origin. Coningsby is bequeathed an extensive and valuable collection of packs of tarots from different eras, some mirroring the political situation of their time. Most remarkable and ancient of all is a pack, possibly in papyrus, traced to early medieval Europe, but rumoured to be made in Egypt. When this pack is produced in the presence of Henry, he recognises its connection with another ancient treasure preserved by his gipsy grandfather, Aaron Lee, in a house on the south downs.

Christmas provides a pretext for the Lees to persuade the Coningsbys to spend a few days in their house, bringing the Egyptian tarot pack with them. After a polite and hospitable welcome, they are brought into a curtained sanctum beyond Aaron's study to see a marvellous set of gold figures which correspond exactly to the cards in Coningsby's pack. They are kept on a table where they move continually in a dance formation by some unknown agency which Aaron vaguely describes as being due to the Earth's magnetic field. At the very centre of the whole the figure of the Fool remains standing perfectly still. The room is suffused with light which changes from one colour of the spectrum to another. It is all very beautiful and delightful, but vast and potentially destructive forces are held there in precarious balance and control. This is threatened by the struggle which develops between the Lees, who desire the Egyptian tarots for themselves, as the combination of cards and figures brings esoteric knowledge and power, and Lothair Coningsby, who looks on his bequest as a link with a dear friend now departed and clings to his possession.

Later in the novel, the Lees unleash a freakish, supernatural snowstorm in which Lothair is nearly overwhelmed, and chaos reigns indoors, as the tarot figures escape from their orderly dance on the table and become dangerous giants on the loose. Nancy and her aunt Sybil are called on to fill heroic sacrificial roles in which love and humility finally prevail over destructive power-seeking. Henry Lee is not damned but changed and, at the end, his marriage looks like going ahead, even though he has in effect attempted the murder of his future father-in-law. Rhoda wants to save the lady of Paradise from the temptations of the snake. She finds herself on the island in the Earth's past where she not only sees that the worship of the evil one is dominating the lives and minds of the inhabitants, but finds that human sacrifices are offered and she is the next one. The whole Psyche myth began with the ceremonial abandonment of the girl on the mountain and Rhoda saw paintings representing this scene on the walls of the beast's castle in the first story. Now she becomes a helpless victim bound on a stone altar, but, as in the myth, the god of love intervenes.

In *Perelandra*, when Ransom has completed his heroic struggle with the diabolic Professor Weston and emerged from caves and tunnels under the mountains to enjoy a heavenly interlude in the company of divine male and female figures, there is discussion of the economy of salvation. Because Maledil, the Christ figure, has lived, died and risen on Thulcandra, Ransom can enact a saving role on *Perelandra*. The two space novels *Out of the Silent Planet* and *Perelandra* belong to a trilogy of which the third is set on Earth and features Ransom, rendered an invalid by his heroic struggles in space, but all the more powerful a spiritual influence for that. *That Hideous Strength* has not been as popular as the first two novels and some, even of Lewis's admirers, have thought it not altogether successful, but it is an attempt to show how the aspirations to mythical worlds in the first two novels have to be applied to the nitty-gritty of life.

That Hideous Strength was strongly influenced by Charles Williams, especially his novel *The Place of the Lion,* which was new not long before Lewis wrote. In the Williams novel a female bluestocking is derided for using her head instead of her feminine intuition and feeling qualities. In *That Hideous Strength* there is a similar character who not only has academic ambitions, but also refuses to have children. This thwarts the mythical purpose of the story, as she is, unknowingly, destined to give birth to a new Arthur, the once and future King who is to save the country at a time of crisis. For this she is berated by Merlin, who comes back as a precursor of the new Arthur. There is a humorous scene in which he talks a language she cannot understand and says that her head should be struck from her shoulders, while she thinks how quaint and sweet he is and smiles peacefully at him. In this novel, Lewis airs his disquiet about the academic life in a university which was the milieu of his own teaching career.

While I have been writing this book, films have been made of Tolkien's *Lord of the Rings* and Rowling's *Harry Potter and the Philosopher's Stone*. These have been satisfying to millions and the first has led many back to the texts of Tolkien's powerful stories of the age-old struggle between good and evil. The success of each of the five Potter novels as it appeared has been phenomenal, and not only with children and those responsible for feeding their minds and keeping them entertained. Humanity on this planet, faced by increasingly perplexing ethical and spiritual problems as we advance into the twenty-first century, is feeling the need to draw on the stored wisdom of the past, as expressed in powerful symbolism and absorbing narrative.

Tolkien has invented another world inhabited by a rich variety of beings of his imagination. It looks back to a past before the environment had become affected and widely urbanised by modern industrial development. With this past we are still connected through what Jung termed the 'collective unconscious'. Concepts of Dragons, Elves, Wizards and so on are not an indulgence in romantic nostalgia, but signify elements and forces still active in our inner life. In *Till We Have Faces*, CS Lewis adopted the genre of historical novel, reconstructing in a twentieth-century manner the world peripheral to ancient Greek culture, from which the Eros and Psyche myth sprang. His concept of Psyche's sister, Orual, is very well Earthed in the preoccupations of a leadership job. JK Rowling's greatest gift is to interweave her mythic material with contemporary life, in a humorous and endlessly inventive way. The Dursleys are caricatures of non-spiritual, selfish living, with their greed and jealousy and horror of anything supernatural. Though Harry loathes this environment and influence, he must start from it and use a series of different devices to attain to the beginnings of non-material understanding represented by Hogwarts School for Wizards and Witches.

In the same way, the folktales collected by Italo Calvino were handed down verbally to preserve the wisdom contained in ancient myth and relate it to the changing conditions of history in which successive generations of human seekers after spiritual growth and progress had to live. They may seem quaint and antiquated now, but before the days of TV and pop culture they enjoyed a popularity comparable with the products of Rowling, Le Guin, Pullman and other such powerful myth builders of our time. There is much talk of a New Age to which the language of traditional religions seems irrelevant to many. Yet there is recognition that the spiritual core of the traditions is still powerful in enabling us to cope with the endless process of adapting ourselves to new developments which seem to throw themselves in our faces with madly increasing velocity. In this situation it is vital to keep alive the pursuit of the arts of music, painting and writing, so that the human spirit may have a space in which to draw on needed resources for sanity and survival. In this sphere the churched and the unchurched may share together the age-old search of the hero or heroine who sets out on a vital quest in the teeth of tremendous odds.

BIBLIOGRAPHY

— ❦ —

Adams, Richard, *The Girl in the Swing,* Penguin Books Ltd., 1980

Allitt, John, article in *Prophecy and Vision*, record of an exhibition on religion and art in Bristol, 1982

Becker, Walt, *Link*, Avon Books Inc., 2000

Berlitz, Charles, *The Bermuda Triangle,* Souvenir Press, 1975

Calvino, Italo, *Italian Tales*, Penguin Books, 1980

Campbell, Joseph, *The Hero with a Thousand Faces,* Paladin Books, 1988

Fidler, J, Havelock, *Ley Lines, Their Nature and their Properties, a Dowser's Investigation*, Turnstone Press Ltd., 1983

Gaarder, Jostein, *The Solitaire Mystery*, Phoenix House, 1990

Hill, Geoffrey, 'Genesis' from *For the Unfallen,* Penguin Books Ltd., 1990

Hyman, Timothy, article in *Prophecy and Vision* (see above under Allitt)

Kelber, Wilhelm, *The Picture of Christ,* The Christian Community Bookshop, 1937

Le Guin, Ursula, *The Left Hand of Darkness,* Orbit, 1969

Lewis, CS, *Out of the Silent Planet*, The Bodley Head, 1978

—— *Perelandra,* Pan, 1960

—— *That Hideous Strength,* Pan, 1955

—— *Till We Have Faces,* Geoffrey Bles, 1956

Luke, Helen, *Through Defeat to Joy, the Novels of Charles Williams in the Light of Jungian Thought,* published privately

Milton, John, *Paradise Lost*

Moore, Thomas, *Care of the Soul,* Piatkus, 1992

Morgan, Marlo, *Mutant Message Down-under,* USA, 1991, distributed by MMCO

Tilby, Angela, *Science and the Soul,* SPCK, 1992

Tolkien, JRR, ed. Christopher Tolkien, *Silmarillion,* George Allen & Unwin, 1977, Unwin Paperbacks, 1979

Warner, Rex, *Stories of the Greeks,* Farrar, Straus Giroux, 1967

Wells, HG, *The War of the Worlds,* Phoenix Mass Markets, 2004

Williams, Charles, *The Place of the Lion,* Gollancz, 1947

—— *The Greater Trumps,* Gollancz, 1932

Printed in the United Kingdom
by Lightning Source UK Ltd.
106976UKS00001B/349-396

9 781844 014224